Pride Publishing books by Bailey Bradford

Single Books
Breaking the Devil
Dark Nights and Headlights
Texas and Tarantulas
Belt Buckles and Cowboy Boots
Something Shattered
Yes, Forever
The Jasper Soul

Southwestern Shifters
Rescued
Relentless
Reckless
Rendered
Resilience
Reverence
Revolution
Revenge
Reluctance
Renounced
Retrograde

Southern Spirits
A Subtle Breeze
When the Dead Speak
All of the Voices
Wait Until Dawn
Aftermath
What Remains
Ascension
Whirlwind

Love in Xxchange
Rory's Last Chance
Miles To Go
Bend
What Matters Most

Ex's and O's
A Bit of Me
A Bit of You
In My Arms Tonight
Where There's a Will
My Heart to Keep

Leopard's Spots
Levi
Oscar
Timothy
Isaiah
Gilbert
Esau
Sullivan
Wesley
Nischal
Justice
Sabin
Cliff

Mossy Glenn Ranch
Chaps and Hope
Ropes and Dreams
Saddles and Memories
Fences and Freedom
Riding and Regrets
Broncs and Bullies
Hay and Heartbreak
Vaqueros and Vigilance

The Vamp for Me
My Life Without Garlic
Don't Stake My Life on It
Sunshine is Overrated
Don't Drink the Holy Water
The Trouble with Mirrors
That's One Cross Vamp

Spotless
Hide
Hunt
Home
Heart

Mystic Tattoos
One Too Many

Coyote's Call
Off Course
In from the Cold
Blue Moon Rising

Valen's Pack
Run with the Moon
Exodus

Calendar Men
Mr. January
Mr. February
Mr. March
Mr. April
Mr. May
Mr. June
Mr. July
Mr. August
Mr September
Mr. October
Mr. November
Mr. December
The 13th Month

Power
Exchange
Submit
Dominate

Wild Ones
Destined Prey
Destined Predator

City Shifters
Bearly There
Harey Situation

Fire and Flutter
Dragon Dreams and Fairy Wings
Wyvern Ways and Elven Magic

Intrinsic Values
Artifacts
Antiques

Hooked on You
In Deep

Anthologies
What's his Passion?: Unexpected Places
What's his Passion?: Unexpected Moments
Racing Hearts: The Lonely Ones

Hooked on You

IN DEEP

BAILEY BRADFORD

In Deep
ISBN # 978-1-83943-740-3
©Copyright Bailey Bradford 2021
Cover Art by Claire Siemaszkiewicz ©Copyright September 2021
Interior text design by Claire Siemaszkiewicz
Pride Publishing

IN DEEP

Dedication

To everyone who wants a summer romance that lasts a lifetime.

Prologue

"Come on, kids, let's see if we can find any shells!" Titus Eisenhower nodded to the parent volunteers forming a human wall between the Pre-K children and the ocean, keeping the kids from getting in past their ankles. The annual field trip to the beach was one of the highlights of the school year for the kids and teachers alike.

Seeing the children's faces lit up with joy, hearing their shrieks of — mostly — laughter, watching them run and splash in the bit of water they could reach...it made his heart swell every single time he got to take part in this trip, and this was his fifth with one of his classes.

The other teachers were at his sides, vigilant, but when it came to children and water, all parents, all *adults*, needed to be watching the whole group.

This year's parents were great. He'd only had one pissed-off dad who had refused to let his child go since he couldn't just hang out with his kid. Other than that, there'd been plenty of parent volunteers, and, wonder of wonders, they got on well, too. Last year, two of the dads had gotten into a fist fight over some perceived insult. *That* had been a disaster.

"God, I bet we don't ever get such a great group of parents again," said Stacy Evans, his best friend and colleague. She'd been hired the same year he had, and they'd become fast friends. Stacy's bright-orange hair was all over the place as the beach breeze whipped it about. She shoved uselessly at several flapping strands. "Why, oh why don't hair ties work for me?"

"Honey, that hair can't be tamed any more than you can," quipped Michelle Ochoa. She was older than Titus and Stacy, but not by too many years. "You're as wild and powerful as the wind."

Michelle was also Stacy's girlfriend, though no one but Titus knew that.

Stacy laughed. "Whatever. When I'm blinded by my own hair, then what'll I do?"

"Mr. Eisenhowew, I finded a shell!" Little Bobby Garza hopped in place as he waved a sandy glob in the air. "Wook!"

Titus grinned and jogged over to Bobby before squatting so he could be eye to eye with the boy. "Hey, you did! That's awesome! Want to dip it in the next wave and see if we can get the sand off?"

"Yes!" Bobby's delighted shriek made Titus' ears ache, but the rest of him filled with sheer wonder and delight. He loved his job, and he loved the kids, loved seeing them grow and learn. It made him less cynical every time he saw the world shine in a child's eyes.

"Then let's do it."

Titus got the other kids to show their treasures. A couple were upset that they didn't find *good* shells, but, overall, everything was going surprisingly well.

After they'd got the kids lined up—and allowed the parent volunteers to take their kids home in their own vehicles, rather than making them ride the buses—Titus took a moment to look back at the ocean. The waves were slight, which was normal for this area of the coast. It was only one-thirty in the afternoon, so the sun was high and bright, the reflection on the water exquisite in its beauty.

"Just think…next weekend, we're going to be here in our own beachfront condo, partying—or relaxing, more likely—for a whole seven days," Stacy said, her soft voice breaking into Titus' quiet appreciation of the view.

Not that he minded. He grinned at Stacy. "You and me and some margaritas," he promised.

Stacy nodded. "Darn right. I'm so looking forward to it."

"Me, too." Titus and Stacy had started their beach tradition their first year at the school. Michelle and Stacy hadn't been dating then. They'd fallen for each other a little over two years ago, but Michelle didn't come to the beach vacations. She had prior commitments with her family in Michigan that took her away.

Titus privately thought Michelle didn't want to intrude, and he had mixed feelings about that. He didn't want to be a third wheel, but he hated to think Stacy might regret Michelle not being there.

"Stop brooding," Stacy said, poking his arm. "You're going to get wrinkles all over your forehead and around your eyes before you hit thirty if you keep doing that."

"I wasn't brooding," Titus protested, immediately trying to smooth out his features.

"Yeah? Then what were you frowning at?" Stacy asked.

"Y'all need to hurry up—we have to get on the road," Michelle called out to them.

"Oops, we're holding everyone up." Titus grinned, relieved at being saved from having to answer Stacy's question.

"I'll keep bugging you until you answer me," Stacy promised as they rushed to the buses.

Titus could have protested, but he knew better. Besides, all he had to do was tell Stacy the truth—he didn't want her to feel like Michelle wasn't welcome.

But he'd keep the other truth to himself—that he was lonely, and when he'd looked out over the water, that sense of loneliness had permeated his happiness, and now, melancholy lingered in the place where joy had been. *Yes, I'll definitely keep that secret.*

Chapter One

"Maybe we should look for jobs here." Stacy gestured with her margarita.

"At Captain's Cove?" Titus asked, knowing full well that wasn't what she'd meant. "But that'd be a waste of our teaching degrees."

"Probably make more money, though." Stacy sipped her drink.

Titus grunted. She kind of had a point.

The server arrived with their entrees.

"Can I get another margarita?" Stacy tossed back the last quarter of her drink. "Please."

The server grinned. "That'll be your third. Your boyfriend'll have to carry you out of here if you drink it as fast as you did the first two. Those suckers sneak up on you. One minute, you're clear-headed, the next, you're trying to dance on the tables, except you can't stand up."

"You calling me a lightweight?" Stacy arched a brow at the server.

He laughed. "Nope, just telling you the truth. Doesn't matter what size you are, what your tolerance of liquor is. The tequila in our margaritas will kick your ass."

Only at the beach would an employee talk so casually to customers. Titus approved.

"Eh. He can drag me out by my ankles if he needs to," Stacy decided. "And he isn't my boyfriend, but he *could* be y —"

"Could you bring some ketchup and sliced lemon please?" Titus cut in, desperate to stop Stacy from outing him. The coastal area they were at was more laid-back than the small town they lived in, but that didn't mean it was safe to be outed, nor was it Stacy's place to do so.

Stacy blinked. "I was *saying*, he *could* be Yolanda's boyfriend if he'd just ask her out. My sister has the biggest crush on him."

Nice save. Stacy was an only child.

The server, who lacked a name tag, rolled his eyes at Stacy. "Sure, that's what you meant." Then he winked at Titus. "Same team, bro. I'm taken, though."

Titus refrained from pointing out that he hadn't made a pass in the first place. "Congratulations." He hoped he sounded sincere.

The server grinned. "Thanks. I'll be back with the liquor, lemons and ketchup."

Stacy reached across the table and touched Titus' arm. "Sorry. Maybe I shouldn't have the third margarita. You drink it."

"I haven't even finished the first, and..." He sighed. "It's fine, Stace."

Stacy shook her head. "No, no it isn't. I almost..." She glanced around, leaned closer, then whispered, "Outed you, and that's bullshit! Especially after—"

"Here we go." The ketchup and lemon slices were set on the table. "The margarita is going to take a few minutes. We've got about a half-dozen in front of you."

"Just cancel it." Stacy sat back. "I think the second one is kicking in anyway."

"Loose tongue, huh?" The server nodded and hustled off.

Stacy glared in his direction. "You know, he's kind of a smart-ass, isn't he?"

Titus laughed. "Stace, eat your shrimp before I snatch them from you."

"Hey," she protested as Titus made a grab for one. "Eat your own damn shrimp!"

They laughed, and Titus was glad to distract her from their previous conversation. Stacy knew almost everything about him, including the one subject he'd told her he never wanted to talk about again. And he was fairly certain she'd been on the verge of bringing it up. Usually, Stacy wasn't such a talkative drunk, but then again, her margaritas were most frequently made with wine, not tequila.

The rest of their meal together was pleasant, and Titus made sure to leave a good tip. He and Stacy walked back to their condo, strolling along the moon-lit beach, chatting about inconsequential things. When they reached the foot of the steps leading to their rented place, Titus stopped. "I think I'm going to sit out here and watch the waves for a bit. Want to join me?"

"Nah, I think I'm going to go in, call Michelle, then pass out. Sheesh, my head's spinning." Stacy grabbed the banister.

"Let me help you upstairs."

It was proof of how intoxicated she was that Stacy didn't protest. He helped her get settled on her bed — she could undress herself once he was out of the room. "Call me if you need me. I've got my phone."

Stacy grunted, and Titus left her to make her call. He trotted out through the door and down the steps, sighing as he reached the last one. He took his shoes off, set them on the flat part of the rail, then leapt off the last step and dug his toes in the sand. Something skittered off to his left. Titus figured it was a little sand crab. If it wasn't, he didn't want to know what it was.

The moon was full, and so bright that he saw spots when he closed his eyes to blink. As far as he could tell, there wasn't a cloud in the sky, just stars and more stars, and that glorious moon.

There was a gentle breeze blowing that kept the humidity from knocking him out. Titus listened to the sound of the waves rolling in. He walked closer to the water, then closed his eyes again. The more he listened, the more musical the waves were. If he let his mind wander, he could imagine some underwater deity having an orchestra of merfolk playing unique instruments thousands of feet below the surface of the water. The sound would just barely reach the open air, a *shush suss, shush suss* of water caressing the sand.

Then his mind drifted to caresses and lovers and how long it'd been since he'd had one, how long since he'd been touched with care or even desire.

"Too long," he whispered, letting the wind carry his words off, along with his peaceful mood. He opened his eyes and blamed the wetness at the corners of them on the wind. Titus gave the waves one last look, then went back to the condo. He'd give himself this one moody night, then he'd relax and enjoy the rest of his vacation.

When he slept that night, he dreamed of wild, whimsical music and waves lapping at his feet.

Chapter Two

The sunlight had barely peeked through the curtains when someone knocked on Titus' bedroom door. "S'minutes."

Well, his tongue wasn't any more awake than the rest of him.

"It's just me," Stacy called out. "Are you decent?"

"Never," Titus snorted, prying his eyes open. "Ugh. What the heck, Stace? It's too early."

Stacy flung the door open. She looked like hell, hair standing up every which way, and bags under her eyes, her hangover apparent. "I gotta go, sweets. I'm sorry, but Michelle just called and she got in a huge fight with her parents over us and she's on the way home and so—"

Titus' stomach dipped. Stacy was going to leave him here, alone?

"I know it's not like she's hurt physically, but emotionally, she's a wreck," Stacy said. "I...I need to be there for her when her plane lands. I love her."

Titus cleared his throat. "Yeah, I—it's fine. You could always bring her here, if you want?"

Stacy bit her bottom lip, and Titus knew what was coming.

"I think I need to spend time with her, just the two of us," Stacy finally replied. "They went off the rails for some reason. Well, could be the new preacher at their church, I guess, and I don't want Michelle to leave me, Titus. I couldn't stand it if she did."

"Go on. I'll be fine, but the offer stands." Titus rubbed at his eyes. "Besides, I can have wild, loud sex once you're gone."

That set Stacy off into a fit of laughter, and Titus flipped her off. "I hope your head pounds all morning."

Stacy stopped laughing long enough to say, "Doesn't hurt. I'm hangover-proof."

Titus thought it wise not to point out her hair or eye bags. He wasn't generally a stupid guy. "Then go pack. I want to get up and piss, and I'm naked. You can't see my junk."

"Ew." Stacy wrinkled her nose. "I don't want to see your junk. I'll shower, then pack, then find you and say goodbye. You're the best, you know?"

"Yeah." *Nope.* Titus began to kick off the sheet.

Stacy shrieked and yelled, "My eyes!" before turning and running out of the room.

Titus got up and stretched. He wasn't sure how he felt about Stacy leaving him alone. Disappointed at first, but maybe it wouldn't be so bad. He could walk around naked if he wanted to, and jack off on the couch—well, not *on* the couch, because he was pretty sure the condo owners would not take kindly to that. But he would have a certain amount of freedom he wouldn't have if he shared the place with someone else.

And who knew? Maybe he *would* get lucky.

Though what that meant, exactly, he couldn't say. He didn't do one-night stands, and he wasn't going to find a long-term lover in the few days he was at the coast. Almost everyone here were tourists anyway.

Titus headed toward the en suite attached to his room. Thinking about dating and sex was not making his morning any better—and that was a sad state of affairs, because thinking about sex *should* have perked at least one part of him up.

But knowing that Stacy would be waiting to tell him goodbye kept Titus from taking a few minutes to jerk off in the shower. He did manage a quick scrub-down before drying and throwing on a pair of swim trunks.

Stacy looked like she'd done a complete one-eighty in the fifteen minutes since he'd last seen her. She was freshly showered, had makeup on and her luggage rested by her left foot as she sipped a cup of coffee. "Slow poke."

Titus groaned and headed for the coffee pot. "It's not fair. You already have coffee."

"You don't even like the stuff," Stacy retorted.

"But I *need* it," Titus grumbled, reaching for a mug. He poured himself some coffee, then added enough sugar and cream to kill the bitter taste.

"That's gross, man," Stacy said. "You just turned your drink into sugared milk."

"Caffeinated sugared milk," Titus corrected. The milk had also cooled the liquid down enough that he could gulp it.

"Look, I really am sorry. I can ask Michelle if she wants to come up tomorrow, but I don't think she will." Stacy did her lip-biting thing again, then continued. "Or maybe she will. She'll feel bad—"

"It's fine," Titus interrupted. "I think maybe it'll do me good to be alone for a few days. Plus I don't have to wear clothes in here."

"Er, okay, if that's a plus…" Stacy took another sip, then set her coffee cup on the counter. "I'm heading out. I *am* sorry. I want to keep our beach tradition going."

"We will." Titus had actually thought it would come to an end—Stacy and Michelle were falling more and more in love every day. They'd be wanting to live their lives together eventually. Although, there were plenty of couples who vacationed together. But if Michelle's family cut her off— That was a horrible thought.

"Don't look so serious," Stacy advised. "Give me a hug. I'll text when I'm home."

Titus set his cup down and folded Stacy into his arms. "Drive safe. Give Michelle a kiss for me."

"Uh, I want a kiss, too." Stacy tipped her cheek toward him.

Titus gave her a smacking peck on it. "Good?"

"Yeah." She picked up her bag, and with a, "Bye," Stacy left the condo.

Titus glanced around at the place. Stacy had been gone ten seconds, and the silence made his ears ring.

"Screw this." Titus grabbed an apple and a bottle of water, then trotted out of the door and down onto the beach.

The sun was barely up, and it was cool out, but not cold. In another couple of hours, it'd be simmering outside. He took a bite of the apple and strolled closer to the water. He kept thinking, of all things, about the Disney character, Moana, and her desire to be out on the water, voyaging away.

Then of course he started singing one of the songs from the movie in between eating his apple. Titus kept his voice soft as a surprisingly peaceful feeling began to steal over him.

Before he knew it, he was wading into the water, taking slow, cautious steps while he stared at the point where the ocean and sky met. The sand gave way quickly under his feet, sucking them down an inch or two if he stood still for very long. He stopped when his knees were covered. The water was warm, and its salt perfumed the air.

He took the last bite of his apple, then tucked the core into his pocket after a quick debate over the legality and ecological consequences of dumping even organic trash in the water. He didn't want to break any laws or harm any sea creatures, so he could deal with the remains being in his pocket.

Titus took another step or two then stopped when he spotted movement not forty or so feet in front of him.

With the sun still not all the way up, he couldn't be sure what he saw — a pelican, maybe, or a dolphin? He squinted. Whatever it was, it wouldn't harm him. Titus resumed his song, daring to sing a little louder. It seemed to him that the breeze supplied perfect backup vocals, whipping around him in time with the tune.

Then he noticed that the thing he'd seen appeared to be closer.

And that there was a fin on it.

A big, scary fin.

That was probably attached to a big, hungry shark.

It was coming right at him.

Titus couldn't even shriek as panic engulfed him. His feet seemed to be stuck in the sand.

Oh, no. That was just him being paralyzed in fear.

Move! Move! Titus shouted in his head. He got one foot up, took a back-step, then did it again, and again—

And figured he was shark bait when his heel landed on something hard and sharp. Titus didn't even have time to shout before he toppled backward.

Chapter Three

Draven smacked Riveen on the shoulder. "You're *such* an asshole."

Riveen snickered and pulled the boogie board under the water. "What? It was funny, and it's not my fault he can't tell the boogie board from a shark fin. Did you see his face?"

Draven whacked his brother again. "Asshole. You're a major—"

Before he could say another word, he and Riveen were tugged under as a wave built up.

Draven and Riveen were strong swimmers. Even with Riveen dragging the boogie board along, it didn't take them long at all to reach the pier a hundred yards away. Draven swiped at the wet hair blotting his vision, gaze immediately aimed in the direction he'd last seen the man Riveen had scared. "Such an *asshole*."

"I think maybe you think I'm an asshole?" Riveen hazarded with enough sarcasm to suffocate the average person as he moved to stand in front of Draven. "Which is odd, 'cause *I* think *you* have a seriously depleted sense of humor."

"Hard to have a sense of humor when my brother's a joke," Draven retorted. Jeez, he'd reverted back to age ten all of a sudden. Riveen had that effect on him.

"Oh, ha ha ha," Riveen drawled. "You're *so* hilarious. You're just mad 'cause I scared off the object of your spank bank material."

Draven spun and had Riveen's head under the water in a heartbeat.

Riveen kicked, and Draven went under a second later. They scuffled for a moment, then shoved away from each other and resurfaced.

"Can you just stop being—?"

"An asshole?" Riveen asked. "Uh, probably not."

Draven nodded. Well, that was an honest answer at least. "He isn't spank bank anything."

"Riiiiiiiight. So you weren't out here last night ogling him?" Riveen snorted. "Dude, I was with you, and I *know* you weren't checking out the woman. Not your type of fish."

"They aren't fish, and we're out here almost every night. Stop making me sound like a stalker."

Riveen splashed Draven. "Stop protesting. It's *because* we're out here together so often that I noticed you drooling over him. Wanna know his name?"

Draven considered trying to drown his brother. Not seriously…for the most part.

"Of course you do. His name is…" Riveen whispered, leaning close. Then he shot back and shouted, "Hey, Titus!"

"Jesus Christ! You ass—" Draven hissed as he spotted the man he'd been looking for before Riveen had been, well, Riveen. And the man—Titus, Draven guessed, because he sure had turned around quickly when Riveen shouted his name — wasn't as far away from them as Draven had expected him to be, which was dangerous. Sound carried over the water, but Draven didn't think Titus was *that* close to them.

"Who's out there?" Titus demanded, shielding his eyes as if the sun, not the moon, were shining brightly. "Who are you?"

"Should I answer him?" Riveen whispered, his voice full of wicked promises.

Draven tore his gaze away from Titus long enough to glare at Riveen. "Why are you doing this?"

Riveen's brilliant smile died away. "Drave, you have to take a chance sometime."

Draven was incensed. "That's for me to decide, isn't it? Not you."

Riveen shook his head. "You'll never do anything but look and lust."

"Who's out there?" Titus asked again, his voice wavering.

"He's going to start to think he was hallucinating or something," Riveen said. "Poor guy."

"You're not pushing me to do *anything*." Draven hated being goaded into something. He resolutely refused to look in Titus' direction again.

Riveen scowled. "You're just going to let that poor guy wonder who yelled his name?"

Draven gave Riveen his own grim smile. "Nope. You are."

"This isn't funny," Titus yelled.

Guilt sucked. Draven hated it. But he wouldn't let Riveen manipulate him. If he let it happen this time, Riveen would forever think he could push Draven to do whatever he wanted.

Draven grabbed Riveen's arm, hard. "Sorry, dude. I'm just a creep named Riveen who saw you out here last night. I have no manners."

Riveen bared his teeth and fisted a handful of Draven's hair. "Fine. I'll go talk to him. He's cute." In a flash, Riveen was free and headed for the shore. "Sorry, man. I know that's creepy, but I'm out here fishing or boogie boarding most nights. Saw you with your friend last night, and she said your name."

Titus stopped twenty feet or so from the water. "That is creepy."

"Yeah. My brother Draven calls me an asshole all the time, but he's a stick in the mud." Riveen kept walking as he talked, and Titus didn't move away.

Draven ducked farther under the pier but glared daggers at Riveen. Why was Riveen being such a dick? Why was he pushing so hard? *Why can't he just let me…?* Draven didn't finish the thought. He took one last look at Titus and ignored the funny dip in his belly. He was going to leave. Let the water envelope him and take him home.

He really *was*. Riveen wouldn't win this battle.

Then Titus laughed—not an entirely comfortable sound, either—at something Riveen said, and Draven fisted his hands.

Riveen held up the boogie board, and Titus' expression shifted from uncomfortable to possibly anger. Draven was betting on irritation at the very least.

He nodded to himself. *Good. Maybe Titus will rip Riveen a new one.*

Except, Riveen was really handsome, and he had that annoying, cheery personality thing going on. Not when it came to Draven, but for everyone else. What would Draven do if Riveen and Titus hooked up?

That thought jarred Draven. He wouldn't do anything. He didn't know Titus and didn't intend to change that.

Draven finally found the strength to slip down into the water, chased by the sound of Riveen's lilting voice.

Draven shifted, and if he moved a little slower than usual as he headed home, it was only because he was enjoying the freedom from his almost ever-present brother.

And he'd keep telling himself that until he believed it.

Chapter Four

Despite what the man who'd called himself Riveen had said, Titus *still* thought he was a creep. Riveen had been handsome, too much so, and perfection had never worked for Titus. As far as he'd seen, there wasn't even a hint of imperfection on Riveen.

"Unless I count his personality." Titus snorted and got into the shower. Riveen was too boisterous, too chirpy and self-assured for Titus. Not that Titus was looking for a guy who was insecure. Riveen, however, radiated a smugness that was off-putting.

And Titus didn't buy his story about the whole name thing. Well, maybe Riveen *had* heard Stacy say his name the night before. That was entirely possible. Titus didn't remember every word of his and Stacy's conversation.

Regardless, he shuddered as he tried to forget about the encounter on the beach. *Riveen's sense of humor sucked, too. Jerk.* Titus firmly shoved the man from his thoughts and grabbed the bar of soap and a washcloth.

He lathered up the cloth, then scrubbed the saltwater from his skin.

Titus luxuriated under the shower for several minutes, letting go of everything except the moment he was in. He touched himself just for the sheer eroticism of it, though he didn't reach for his cock to jack off. There was something to be said for anticipation — and he definitely felt a sense of *that*, though he couldn't have said why.

When the water began to run cool, he tipped the showerhead down, keeping the chilled water off him, then poured out a palmful of conditioner. Slowly, so exquisitely slowly and perfectly, he began to spread the conditioner over his hard dick. After so many minutes of caressing himself, not letting himself think, only feel, Titus' imagination sprang to life.

He didn't control it, or try to, just let the visions flash behind his closed lids as he fisted his hand around his length to begin a leisurely stroke.

With his other hand, Titus cupped his balls. In his mind's eye, there was a rough, bigger hand on his shaft, a matching one fondling his nuts. He could picture glimpses of dark brown, maybe even inky black irises staring at him, big eyes, narrow nose, thick eyebrows drawn together — but he didn't envision an entire face.

That was okay. He gasped as pleasure coursed from his cock and balls to all points throughout his body. Titus tipped his head back and propped one foot on the side of the shower stall. That gave him access to move his fingers past his balls, to trail them back and forth over the soft skin behind his sac while he twisted his other hand around the head of his dick.

Little sparks shot out over his fantasy man, reds and golds bursting from the corner of his imaginary lover before fading away. Titus slipped his fingers even farther and teased them over his hole as he jacked himself a little faster. Masturbating felt good, but how much better would it be to have someone actually there with him, watching him, encouraging him — touching him?

It'd been so long since Titus had been touched, been loved, made love to, that he almost couldn't remember what it felt like. Maybe he never really had known how it would feel to be more than just some guy's piece of ass. He'd thought, once upon a time, that someone had cared, but —

Titus shut down that train of thought and focused on making himself feel good. He tightened his grip on his cock and played with the bundle of nerves under the cap, making himself whimper.

Hands, oh god, to have hands on me other than my own, holding me in place, holding me up, pushing fingers into me — Titus did just that, pushed two wet fingers into his ass, and gasped. *Oh, but if they weren't mine* — He tried to bring up his fantasy man again. Those dark eyes would hold him still as sure as any hands ever would.

Titus stroked his cock faster and moved his fingers inside himself, small thrusts, nothing too taxing on him considering how he was positioned and his limited reach.

He thought of someone else, with better access, pushing deeper into him, stretching him wider with more fingers, a promise of everything in eyes so black that they would have smothered even the stars.

Titus cried out. He wanted that, wanted to be consumed in lust by someone, with someone, for someone.

But he wasn't, and suddenly all that rushing pleasure he'd felt came crashing to a halt. Titus kept his eyes closed and tried to focus on his hands, his fingers, his cock and balls and ass—but when he finally came, he was underwhelmed by the experience.

Goddamn it! He was lonely. He was tired of getting himself off. He was tired of being, much like Riveen's maligned brother—*Draven? Yeah, him*—a stick in the mud.

Riveen would have propositioned him, if Titus had given him a few more minutes. Titus had known it as sure as he'd known he was standing out on the beach, talking to a guy he didn't particularly like.

But did he have to like someone to fuck them? Normally, yes, he did. Titus shut the water off and stepped out of the shower stall. He sucked at one-night stands, or he had. Even so, surely getting off with a stranger would be better than a mediocre orgasm in the shower?

After toweling off and brushing his teeth, Titus put on a good layer of deodorant—the humidity did him no favors in the sweating department—and left the bathroom. He found another pair of shorts to put on, but hesitated. What was he doing? It was late. He didn't need to get dressed. There was nowhere to go.

The tug of the beach pulled at his gut, but Titus ignored it. He didn't want to risk running into Riveen. Not that a guy who looked as handsome as Riveen would be waiting around hoping to get laid by Titus.

Titus snorted at himself. He was on vacation. Usually, he and Stacy just relaxed and ate out, hit up the beach. Maybe it was time to shake up his routine. Step out of his comfort zone.

Get laid.

Titus took a shaky breath, then made a decision. He was going to have a *real* vacation. A wild, crazy, sex-filled — well, okay, maybe just one sexual experience with someone else vacation to remember.

He wasn't going to be a stick in the mud, not for the next few days.

Chapter Five

"Oh-ho! Look who came out to play!"

Titus winced and wished he didn't have to turn around. He'd much rather ignore Riveen, pretend he didn't hear him, but the club he was in was practically dead. Plus, Titus' mom would have boxed his ears for being rude. His manners were firmly ingrained in him.

That didn't mean he spun around in a hurry. *Go out, I tell myself. Have fun, get laid, be wild – and I run into the one man on the planet I know I would never be attracted to.*

Still, Titus plastered on a smile as he faced Riveen. "Hey, er, Riveen. How's it going?"

Riveen dog-whistled him and all but eye-fucked Titus at the same time. "Oh, yum yum! Don't you look deliciously fuckable?"

"You're asking me?" Titus retorted, holding his bottle of beer a little tighter. He didn't hate Riveen, didn't know him well enough for any strong emotion, but he just wasn't interested, despite the fact that Riveen was sex on two nicely muscled legs.

Riveen giggled. "It was a rhetorical question, duh." He gestured toward the dance floor. "It's dead here tonight, but that just means we can dance until we drop, if you want."

Titus took a drink of his beer. He wanted to dance. In fact, he *loved* dancing. He just didn't get to do it very often, not with another man.

"Aw, come on, you're gonna give me a complex," Riveen wheedled. "I'm not asking to fuck, just dance. There's only four other guys here, and one of them is my cousin, so he's a no. The other three are into stuff I'm not."

Titus widened his eyes at Riveen. "There are things you aren't into?"

Riveen flipped him off while laughing. "Yes, there are, like not using condoms. I'm totally not into that, PrEP or not."

Titus shuddered. "Yeah, no." He chugged the rest of his beer. Riveen was exaggerating—there were more people there, but not many. What would it hurt to dance with Riveen? As long as he was up front about everything. "Just dancing, though."

"Of course, St. Titus."

Titus probably should have been offended by that, but Riveen fluttered his lashes and was so outrageous in his enunciation, it was impossible to miss that he was joking.

"Lead the way." Titus nodded, wondering if Riveen was going to out-dance him. It was possible. Titus was rusty and he wasn't an amazing dancer. He knew how to have fun…or he used to.

Riveen whipped his phone from his pants pocket— Titus had no idea how the phone fit in that pocket to begin with. Riveen's pants looked painted on. "Let me just send this—"

Before Titus could object, Riveen took his picture.

"Hey, what the hell?" Titus growled, trying to decide whether or not to yank the phone from Riveen's hand. "You don't just take a person's photo without asking!"

"Uh, I think it's legal, but whatever." Riveen shrugged. "It's a safety precaution. Sent it to a friend. I don't know you."

Titus would have snapped at Riveen some more, but he did have a point. Sort of. "We aren't leaving here together. *All* we're doing is dancing. That's it. Nothing else."

Riveen sighed. "Fine. I'm a really excellent fuck, though. Bet I can change your mind."

Titus took a step back, shaking his head. "Listen to me, Riveen. I said no. I meant no."

Riveen actually blushed and ducked his head. "I didn't mean I'd make you have sex with me. Jeez."

"Then accept that I absolutely *won't* have sex with you, and we can dance." Titus wondered why he was being so obstinate about this—himself, not Riveen. After all, hadn't he promised himself a good time, and at least one sexual encounter? And here he had a man as handsome as Riveen all but spreading for him... Titus couldn't make any sense of it.

Riveen smiled. "Fine. Let's dance. I promise to keep my hands to myself."

Titus followed him to the dance floor just as a song that was more bass than anything else began playing. Titus let the beat take him, let his body move and roll with the rhythm.

He couldn't help but notice that Riveen wasn't a very good dancer. He shuffled and moved his hips, flapped his hands now and then. Titus was petty enough to find relief in Riveen not being perfect after all.

Regardless of Riveen's lack of talent, Titus danced with him through several songs. He was aware of more people joining them on the floor, of the sweat running down his own back, his forehead. Titus swiped at his brow and kept moving, almost closing his eyes, lost in the joy of dancing.

Riveen's not-so-soft curse snapped him out of that reverie.

"Son of a bitch!"

Titus opened his eyes all the way and looked at Riveen, who was grinning like a lunatic and staring at another man.

A tall, gangly man with thick, shoulder-length dark hair. *Black or brown?* Titus couldn't tell in the disco-lighted club. He liked the loose-limbed way the man walked, the way he seemed to ignore everyone around him, as if he were alone in the building, except for the glare…that stern expression that was directed at Riveen.

Titus stopped dancing. "You have a boyfriend you're trying to make jealous?"

Because Titus would be fucked if he was going to get into a fight over Riveen.

Riveen cackled and grabbed his hand. "Oh no, honey. That's my brother, Draven. I didn't think it would work, but what do you know? Here he is."

"What would work?" Titus asked, jerking his hand back. "What game are you playing?"

Draven's glance shifted to Titus, and even in the dim light, even with the distance, he could make out the brilliant green color of Draven's eyes.

Titus' heart and dick thumped almost in synch with one another. Draven wasn't perfectly handsome like Riveen. He was closer to average in looks, except for those gorgeous eyes.

Titus had never seen eyes like that before.

"My job here is almost done," Riveen said. "It would have been totally done if you'd just held my hand."

Titus barely heard Riveen. He was too focused on Draven.

And Draven showed no sign of seeing anyone else except Titus.

Chapter Six

Draven knew his brother was manipulating him, and yet, he'd been helpless to prevent it. From the moment Riveen had texted and sent him a photo of Titus looking sexier than sin and ready for fucking, Draven had been hooked by his brother's scheme.

Yes, Draven wanted Titus. And, damn it all, Riveen was insistent on provoking Draven into taking action.

Riveen knew him too well. After the beach incident, Riveen had spent hours talking to anyone who would listen about how handsome and funny and sexy Titus was.

And also talking to someone who didn't want to hear it — Draven.

Draven's dreams had been filled with images of Titus. Not innocent ones, either.

Even so, Draven had been determined to stay away from him.

Then Riveen had sent the picture of Titus wearing black jeans that were so tight, they looked painted on. The shirt Titus wore accentuated his lean chest, and something in Titus' expression had made him seem searching, hungry…although Draven was probably only projecting.

Except now he didn't think that was the case. Titus had stopped dancing, and Riveen, beaming like a fucking lunatic, shimmied his ass over to another man.

Draven didn't know what to say as he came to a halt in front of Titus.

Titus gulped and twin streaks of pink blossomed on his cheeks. He glanced to where Riveen had been, then returned his gaze to Draven's.

"Want to dance?" Titus asked, his voice barely audible over the racket blaring through the speaker system.

Draven nodded and decided to be bold. He wasn't a blushing virgin.

Well, Titus was blushing, but Draven didn't think that meant *he* was a virgin either.

Before he could let his brain babble on, Draven moved closer to Titus. He ignored the way his hand trembled as he dared to grip Titus' hip.

But he couldn't ignore the way Titus gasped, or the heat coming off the man in waves. Draven slipped his other hand around to Titus' back, his gaze still locked with Titus', and with a tug, brought their bodies together.

He'd seen Titus dance, the way Titus let the music flow through him, much like the way Titus' need flowed into Draven.

Draven's cock began to harden within seconds. He ignored that unruly part and began to move with Titus, dancing close despite the fast tempo, at least until the song finished.

Titus fit in his arms, against his body, like they were made for each other. The rigid press of Titus' cock against Draven's hip was proof that Draven's lust was returned equally. He tightened his grasp on Titus' hip and used his other hand to press Titus closer. Then they were grinding, together every other step before Draven spun Titus out—not far, because of *course* Riveen was in the way.

Titus came back into Draven's arms like a dream. As tempting as it was to hold on to him. Draven didn't. Dancing was something Draven enjoyed and was good at, and Titus was his match on the floor.

And likely in bed, or over the counter, or on the beach –

Draven grunted and pushed aside the thoughts. He wanted—no, *needed*—this time, this freedom to be sensual and ride the rhythm of the music.

Titus seemed to need it, too, smiling slightly as he kept in step with Draven.

Then the music slowed, and Draven had Titus up against him again, this time with Titus' back to his chest.

Titus made a purring sound and leaned his head against Draven's shoulder and ground his ass against Draven's cock.

Draven slipped both hands around Titus' waist and teased at the band of his jeans. Despite the pants being so tight, they had enough stretch to them that Draven could slip his fingertips under that band, could feel hot skin, hard muscles and the brush of pubic hair.

He pressed, encouraging Titus to grind faster against him. Draven bit back a gasp at the erotic heat that flicked up from his groin to spread throughout his body. He was dangerously close to coming in his pants.

Even so, he wasn't pushing Titus away. Draven worked his hands down a little farther and felt what he was seeking — the silky, hard ridge of Titus' cock.

Titus jolted and gasped before turning his head and sucking on Draven's neck.

Draven tensed, fighting the need to come. He wouldn't lose his shit on the dance floor with Riveen gawking at them, and Draven *knew* Riveen was watching.

Draven ran his fingertips over the wet tip of Titus' cock. He canted his head and hoped Titus would hear him. "Take me home. I want to fuck you."

Draven didn't doubt it was what Titus wanted as well, or some version of that. Draven was versatile — he'd bottom with pleasure for Titus.

But Titus went still for a moment, and Draven wondered how he'd managed to so badly misread him.

Then Titus shivered and made Draven's heart beat again. "Let's go."

Chapter Seven

"My place," Titus suggested, so nervous that he was trying not to let his teeth chatter. He was hornier than he was nervous, though. "Unless yours is closer?" He was testing, seeing if Draven knew where he lived, too, because Riveen had mentioned a brother that night on the beach.

Draven tugged him toward the club exit. "My house is across the street. Close enough?"

"Across—" Titus knew his eyes were huge, but the homes across the street were beach-side mansions with the occasional vacation rental stilt-home here and there.

"Yes." Draven didn't seem to be one for words, and Titus felt a flicker of worry that he was making a mistake by leaving with the man.

Then Draven turned and looked over his shoulder, and the hot, molten need in his gaze annihilated Titus' worries. Draven gave just the barest hint of a smile, and Titus would have followed him anywhere at that point.

They exited the club, and Draven kept hold of Titus' hand as they walked to the curb.

"I'm not a danger to you," Draven said. "You looked worried."

"I don't do this," Titus admitted, feeling himself blush. "I haven't even, well..." Pride warred with honesty. "I haven't even been with anyone in years, okay? So I'm —" Draven's cupping his jaw startled him into silence.

Titus looked into Draven's jewel-bright eyes and went warm through and through. He forgot to breathe for a second, then exhaled slowly as Draven leaned in.

The kiss was soft, chaste, a brush of lips, but Titus shivered and whimpered before he could stop himself.

Draven rumbled, then used his grip on Titus' head to tilt it slightly, and the kiss went from chaste to possessive, hot and searing as Draven licked into Titus' mouth.

Titus couldn't have stopped himself from responding and moving closer if his life had depended on it — and considering where they were, it might have done so.

Draven at least had the sense to keep the kiss short, because two men kissing in Texas, even in the area they were in, were at risk of harm. They both knew it. Draven rumbled again as he moved back. "When I get you home, I won't stop with a kiss."

Jesus. You'd better not! Titus didn't trust himself to speak the words. He settled for a nod, then Draven and he checked for cars before they jogged across the roadway.

And Titus suddenly felt young and foolish, carefree and daring, as if each step he took shed responsibilities and fears he'd carried for as long as he could remember.

The memory of the last time he'd done anything sexually adventurous tried to creep in on his joy, but

Titus kicked it aside. He'd been held down by that weight for years. He was tired of being uptight and not living life to its fullest.

And he really wanted to have sex with Draven.

Who led him to one of the stilted beach houses rather than a mansion. Titus sighed in relief. "Thought you were a billionaire or something there for a minute. Not that these stilted places are cheap, but—"

"My family has owned property here for generations," Draven said. "We've always lived by the water."

"Must be nice." Titus smiled to show he wasn't being snarky.

Draven's gaze went right to his mouth. "Convenient." He tugged Titus in front of him. "After you."

Titus was at the base of the wooden steps. He knew Draven would be ogling his ass, and that was fine with Titus. He started up the steps and heard Draven curse.

Titus chuckled. It was so good to be wanted, lusted after, seen.

Draven's footsteps sounded behind him as Titus hit that middle of the stairway. He sped up and laughed when Draven did the same. By the time he reached the landing, Draven was all but on him.

A second later, Draven had Titus in his arms and had spun him around. Titus' back hit the door with Draven's hands cushioning the blow. Draven sucked Titus' bottom lip, and Titus clutched at him and moaned.

When he made that needy sound, Draven slipped his tongue inside Titus' mouth and white-hot lust sparked along every nerve ending in Titus' body. He curled his hands into fists, grabbing handfuls of Draven's shirt, then pulled, jerking it from his pants.

Titus slid his tongue alongside Draven's while letting go of the material in his hands and instead reaching for the warm skin he'd gained access to.

Draven had a little bit of hair on his abs, just enough to make Titus even more eager to get him naked.

Titus' cock throbbed as Draven sucked on his tongue while simultaneously slipping one thick thigh between Titus' legs.

Draven moved his hand from Titus' jaw to his neck, and Titus shivered, trying to get closer to Draven. Draven's hard prick nudged Titus' hip. Titus wasn't the only one verging on desperation.

He ran his hands around to Draven's back, then burrowed them under the waistband of his jeans. Draven was going commando, and Titus nearly came on the spot as he found himself palming the firm swells of Draven's ass.

Draven did his rumbling thing again and rutted faster against Titus.

Titus nipped Draven's tongue then turned his head aside.

Draven didn't hesitate.

Titus couldn't hold back the hungry sound he made when Draven began kissing and sucking on his neck.

Titus could have a few marks, a few mementos of this night to look at. He might even take pictures and save them.

That was as far as his thought process got before Draven sucked on the tender skin under his ear. Titus grabbed at Draven's ass, urging him to do...more. More of everything.

Draven got a hand between them and cupped Titus' cock through his jeans. He squeezed, and Titus cried out.

"Inside," Draven rasped, and whether he meant he wanted to get inside Titus or inside the house, or any mix of those, Titus didn't know or care.

Draven moved, the door opened and they tumbled inside.

Titus had his mouth on Draven's before the door even shut. Draven pulled, and down they went, a tangle of limbs and lust sprawling on the floor.

Titus didn't know who took off what, how they managed to do it — nothing. He only knew the press of Draven's skin and bulk over him and the press of Draven's solid, thick cock into him, with the hard floor beneath him no competition for the hard man above him.

Draven kept kissing him, kept touching and rubbing, and Titus was going to come just from that. He wouldn't have minded, but he wanted more.

"Please," he managed between burning kisses. "In me." He couldn't quite force himself to ask more bluntly.

Draven licked Titus' bottom lip, kissed his neck, then knelt between his legs. "Are you sure?"

Titus nodded, trying not to gulp as he looked at Draven's cock. His toys weren't even that big.

"You said it's been a while," Draven said, his voice rough as sand on skin.

"With anyone else," Titus clarified. "I have — toys," he forced out.

Draven nodded and leaned over to grab his pants. He pulled out a strip of condoms.

Titus' cheeks burned. He must have seemed like an easy lay—*and why feel bad about that? I'm an easy lay, tonight. There's nothing wrong about that. Nothing at all. It's normal.*

Draven opened one of the packages then rolled the condom down his length. He stroked it a couple of times as he looked at Titus.

Titus caught on to his hesitation. "As long as those are lubed, we're good. Just...just fuck me." That hadn't been as hard to say as Titus had expected it to be. "Just go slow at first." He liked the burn, the stretch, the pain that preceded the pleasure, even if he was using a dildo.

Draven nodded once, then lowered himself over Titus, one hand on his prick, the other planted beside Titus' head.

Titus bent his legs, then decided, *screw it*, and wrapped them around Draven's hips.

"Yeah," Draven whispered, the tip of his cock nudging Titus' hole. "Pull when— fuck!"

Titus hissed and arched as he kept up the pressure on Draven, encouraging him to keep going, to push the fat head into him. The burn was blended perfectly with pleasure, and Titus had the fleeting thought that he'd been crazy to wait so long to do this with another man again.

Draven's breath gusted from him as he gritted his teeth, then Titus pushed, and in went the crown, spreading him, making him ache and want in sweet perfection.

Titus slipped his arms around Draven's neck. "Come here," he slurred.

Draven lowered himself down as he rocked gently, working his cock into Titus' ass.

Titus quivered all over, inside and out. He parted his lips for Draven's kisses, and did something he hadn't thought he'd ever be able to do—he let go, stopped thinking and just felt, let Draven fill him slow and steady.

When Draven was buried as deeply as he could go, Titus moaned and dug the blunt tips of his fingers against Draven's back. *Go, go, go!*

Draven withdrew almost all the way, then sank his dick back into Titus. He didn't remain still, didn't revel in the moment.

Titus didn't want him to. That aching stretch would fade, and he wanted to feel everything, *now*.

As if he knew Titus' thoughts, Draven began thrusting harder, pulling out completely, giving Titus' rim more stimulation as he penetrated him over and over again.

Each time Draven thrust into him, he did so harder than the time before.

Titus arched and moaned, cursed and begged. He'd never been a vocal lover, but he couldn't be anything else, the way Draven fucked him. Every part of Titus felt alive and needy, aroused and teetering on the edge of a release that would rival any others.

Draven panted and bucked harder, raising his lips from Titus', mouth open, jaw slack.

Titus' vision blurred, ecstasy building up, coiling tightly in his ass as Draven rubbed the head of his cock over Titus' gland with every thrust. He shoved a hand between them and fisted his own shaft. Titus didn't even need to jack himself, just the tight squeeze of his hand around his dick was enough to send him spiraling into climax.

He heard a shout that reverberated in his skull when bliss washed over him in waves. Draven's cock was deep inside him, with Draven jerking his hips frantically.

There had never been a more perfect moment in time, in life — that was all Titus knew before he was lost for long, long minutes in his own orgasm.

But reality had to seep back in. *Ugh. How did I manage to forget this awkwardness?* Titus stared up at the ceiling as Draven lay panting beside him. Titus' own breathing hadn't evened out yet, and already he felt out of place and incapable of handling his departure with any dignity.

How does one have dignity hunting down one's clothes, in a house one has never been to before, with a stranger —

"Shower?"

Titus blinked. "Huh?"

Draven sat up and yawned, and Titus thought there was his excuse to leave.

But Draven seemed to have other ideas. "Want to shower?" Then he shook his head. "No. How about a swim?"

"In the ocean?" Titus winced. *Obviously*, Draven had meant the ocean.

"Yeah. We can shower after. I find the ocean..." Draven blushed for some odd reason. "Reviving."

Titus sat up and laughed. "Well, yeah. That salt water in your eyes wakes you up."

Draven surprised him by chuckling. The sound warmed Titus to his core.

"So that's a yes?" Draven asked, turning his pretty gaze Titus' way.

"Sure. I don't have trunks," Titus said, but Draven waved off his concern.

"This part of the beach is private," Draven explained. "I don't usually wear anything when I swim at night, but I can grab you a pair of shorts if you want?"

Titus could easily imagine getting arrested for indecent exposure, private beach or not. "Er, I think I'd feel more comfortable in shorts, if that's okay."

"It is." Draven got to his feet, and Titus looked him over once, then a second time more slowly.

"Wow, you're perfect," he muttered, much to his embarrassment. Titus scrambled up off the floor. "Uh, that wasn't very cool of me. I...well, suck at this whole one-night-stand thing." He glanced at the floor where they'd fucked. "Part of why I haven't been with anyone in so long."

Draven cupped Titus' chin and nudged so that Titus raised his eyes to Draven's. He ran his thumb over Titus' lips. "How long are you here for?"

Titus' heart seemed to skip a beat. "Uh...a-a few more days. Five at most."

"Then..." Draven pressed on Titus' lip.

Titus opened his mouth.

And Draven kissed him, just like Titus was hoping he would, all heat and hunger and lust.

Titus slipped his hands around to Draven's ass and held on while he plundered Draven's mouth as eagerly as Draven plundered his.

Despite being fully aroused, Titus didn't complain when Draven moved back and said, "Beach. Water. Come with me."

Titus forgot about the shorts, but Draven didn't. "Trunks."

Titus watched Draven lope past him, watched the rounded swells of Draven's ass flex as he moved, the pads of his feet as they were bared when he took a step. Draven was a treat to see.

Draven wasn't gone long enough for Titus to feel awkward again. He handed Titus a pair of black board shorts.

When Titus took them, Draven waited by the back door while he put them on.

Draven cleared his throat when Titus pulled the shorts up. Titus gave him an expectant look.

Draven glanced at him then away. "I, ah. I was going to say, before I kissed you. Since you don't do one-night stands, maybe this could be a five-night stand?" He blushed once more, this time darkly.

Titus' heart did that stupid thing again where it soared in joy. "W-we could do that. Five nights after this one."

"And maybe the days too?" Draven rushed out, finally locking gazes with Titus, though he shifted his weight from foot to foot, which Titus thought was a sign of nervousness. He also thought Draven sexy, and adorable in his awkwardness. "I'd like that."

Draven's smile was breathtaking. He nodded and opened the door. "Ready to swim?"

Titus closed the distance between them. "Not going to have your brother show up disguised as a shark, are we?"

Draven's blush returned. "Not as a shark, no. Er, not as anything. He'd better not turn up, is what I mean."

"I think that's asking too much of him for the entire five nights," Titus pointed out.

"And days," Draven added when Titus passed him to walk out the door. "And you're right. You seem to know Riveen well."

"He's pretty see-through," Titus agreed. *Like a shallow tide pool.* Draven was deeper, like the ocean caressing the sand right outside past the steps. "Oh, this is nice."

"I think so." Draven gestured. "No one on the beach but us."

"Hmm." Titus thought about the things they could do on the beach.

And what a pain it'd be to get sand out of their crooks and creases. "Swim?"

Draven chuckled. "Swim." He took Titus' hand, and together they ran into the warm waves.

Titus shrieked when something brushed his leg, but Draven just called out, "Seaweed!" and kept tugging on his hand, so Titus decided to let go and enjoy the time he had with this intriguing man, with the beach their playground and the glorious moonlight casting bright reflections on the water.

Chapter Eight

Five nights left

Draven ticked the day off in his head. He'd been a little nervous about proposing four or five days and nights spent together, but he was glad he'd spoken up. Titus had a life and job and home somewhere else. It wasn't like he and Draven were going to run off and get married.

This was just a vacation affair for Titus, and Draven was totally fine with that. He'd be a fool to pass up a chance to enjoy it. Titus was sexy, smart and funny. Draven had been alone for a long time…and there was an exceedingly good chance he'd be alone for a long time once Titus went home.

Draven heard his front door open and groaned. "Riveen, go away!" Titus would have knocked. So would anyone else, but Riveen always barged right in.

"What? You know I'm here for all the down and dirty details of your hookup!" Riveen leered as he propped a shoulder against the bathroom doorframe.

"Ohh, you're getting all prettied up! Are you seeing Titus tonight? Gonna get laid, round two?"

More like round five. Not that Draven was going to share that with his brother. "Titus and I spent the day on the *U.S.S. Lexington*," Draven said, glaring at his brother before looking at himself in the mirror again. He looked as good as he was going to get, so he turned and headed for the door. "Move, Riv."

"Not until you tell me all about the sex!"

Draven rolled his eyes and poked Riveen in the armpit.

"Ack!" Riveen shrieked and scrambled away. "Fuck you! That's cheating!"

Draven stalked him down the hallway, wiggling his fingers at Riveen menacingly. "How's it cheating? All's fair in the battle of the brothers."

Riveen's mouth dropped open, though he kept moving backward, into the living room. "Oh, my gods! Who are you and what have you done with my brother? You know, the one that's had a stick up his ass ever since he turned twenty or so and thought he had to be boring to be an adult."

"Fuck off," Draven retorted. He lunged, and Riveen shrieked again, turned to bolt—and flipped over the couch.

The thud when he hit the floor in front of the piece of furniture was oddly comforting. Or maybe not so oddly, considering what a pest his brother could be.

"I didn't even touch you," Draven said when Riveen started cussing him. "Not my fault you panicked and acted without thinking."

"Oh, hey, there you are, Drave." Riveen got to his feet. "I figured you couldn't repress the uptight part of yourself for long."

Draven started to snap at Riveen, but honestly, he'd actually been having fun with his brother for the first time in…far too long. He kept his irritated expression in place as he jumped over the couch and bounced off the seat cushions.

"Oh my gods! Ack!" Riveen yelled and took off for the kitchen.

Draven pounced and tackled his brother before he made it past the sink.

"Going to come over and pester me, eh?" he muttered before he began poking at Riveen. He didn't tickle, exactly, just poked.

His brother shrieked and squirmed—and laughed, like he hadn't laughed with Draven since they'd been kids.

What happened to us? Draven really didn't need to ask. He knew what had happened.

"Oh gods, I'm gonna peeeeeeee," Riveen declared as he thumped Draven's throat with a finger. "Get offa me!"

Draven hesitated.

Which was his mistake.

Riveen cackled when he flipped Draven onto his back. "Sucker!" He went for Draven's armpits.

Draven huffed and slapped at the jerk's hands. "Not happening. I'm not ticklish, dork."

"Yeah, that's right," his brother muttered, trying to capture Draven's wrists. "But I bet you like having all that chest hair. Shame if you had a bald spot…"

Draven bucked and twisted. He wasn't letting anyone yank out his chest hair.

Riveen toppled to the side but sprung up and darted backward, laughing. "Hah! Whatever Titus did to you, I totally approve!"

"He didn't—" Draven began, but someone knocked.

"Adios!" Riveen ran for the back. "See you later, dork."

Draven rushed to the front. He wasn't expecting anyone other than Titus. He opened the front door, and Titus smiled then frowned.

"Um. Were you wrestling a bear or something? I heard noise and shouts when I was on the steps but I thought it was the TV," Titus said. "Now I'd guess your brother is here?"

Draven ran a hand through his hair—which seemed to be standing on end—and stepped back so Titus could come in. "Yeah, Riveen wanted to know if I got laid last night," Draven admitted. "I managed to distract him."

Titus' expression took on a wistful air. "Ah. That must be a brother thing. I'm an only child."

"Sibling thing, probably," Draven guessed. "Come on in."

Titus stepped inside. "I'm glad you and Riveen have each other."

"Oh, we have six more brothers, and six sisters," Draven said before he thought about it. Titus looked stunned. "Uh. Mom and Dad obviously didn't bother with birth control." Not that there was such a thing for their kind. "And they wanted a big family."

"Fourteen kids?" Titus squeaked. "That's…that's a lot."

"Well, they had us over a course of about thirty years." Draven wanted to slap himself. Why was he being so chatty—and honest? "So we aren't all close in age. Riveen and I are in the middle, actually. Well, we're kids six and seven. So. Yeah."

"Wow. Family get-togethers must be awesome." Titus definitely sounded wistful.

Draven took him by the hands and pulled him closer. "If by awesome you mean filled with a bunch of screaming babies and toddlers, and yeah, siblings, then they certainly are." And before he could let himself say anything else that he shouldn't, Draven took a kiss, then another one, then a third still as he wrapped his arms around Titus.

Yes, they'd spent the day together, then parted ways to get cleaned up and ready for a night out—dinner, a movie, a walk on the beach. Draven had already come once with Titus before they'd headed off to see the U.S.S. *Lexington*, but that seemed like days ago rather than hours.

He wanted Titus again already.

Draven had plans, though. He eased out of the kiss and released Titus only far enough so he could look Titus over. "Damn. You are one sexy fucker."

Titus blushed. "Thanks. You too."

Draven brushed the backs of his knuckles over Titus' fair hair. "I like this without stuff in it. It looked good earlier, but this is better. I can run my fingers through it." And he did so, which had Titus' eyelids fluttering closed as he moaned softly.

"Damn, Titus. You keep making those sounds and looking so sexy, we won't make it out of the house," Draven muttered.

"I don't mind if we stay in," Titus rasped. "Can order pizza..."

Draven shook his head. "We'll go out and let the anticipation build. When we get back here, I'm going to spend all night fucking you."

Titus shivered. "Please, yes."

Draven kissed him again. "I want to enjoy an evening out with you. I think we both need it."

"Okay. I'd like that." Titus licked his lips. "Uh. Your hair is...is big?"

Draven felt his hair and laughed. "Oh, yeah. It is. The humidity, along with a wrestling match with Riveen. That'll do it."

Titus laughed, and Draven brought him farther into the house.

He liked Titus' laugh. In fact, he liked everything he knew about the man so far. It was a good thing they'd only be spending the next handful of days and nights together, otherwise he might end up with a broken heart.

Chapter Nine

Four nights left

Titus told himself that was plenty of time. It was a vacation fling, after all. Before he knew it, he'd be back at home, reading up on new teaching methods and working on a budget for school suppliers.

He wouldn't get attached to Draven. He couldn't possibly in the short time they had together.

It didn't matter that Draven had turned out to be funny and kind, smart and sexy —

Well, I wouldn't be having this fling with him if he wasn't all those things. Titus propped himself up on one elbow and stared down at Draven as he slept. There was enough moonlight coming in through the curtains for Titus to see Draven's features.

He looked softer in sleep, younger, with the moonlight bringing a glow to his tan skin. Titus wanted to touch him, but he didn't want to wake Draven. He *did*, but he wouldn't.

Despite his shower earlier, Draven still smelled like the ocean — salty and wild. Titus loved the way Draven's skin was warm and scented like the Gulf Coast. Maybe it was because Draven liked to be in the water so much. Every day they'd been in the ocean at least twice. Titus guessed Draven was such a natural in the water because he'd always lived by it. He could dive under and hold his breath for long periods of time. Titus had freaked when Draven did that the first time.

Draven moved through the water like he was half-fish. *Merman, maybe.* Titus grinned down at him, his fingers itching to touch Draven.

Four nights. We have four more nights.

How much sleep did they really need?

"Can feel you watchin' me."

Titus squeaked and almost fell off the bed. Draven grabbing his arm was the only reason that didn't happen.

"Jesus!" Titus gasped and flopped onto his back. "Don't *do* that to me!"

"Do what?" Draven kicked the sheet off. "You were watching me sleep."

Titus closed his eyes. "That makes me sound like a creep."

Draven rolled on top of him, although he didn't let all his weight rest on Titus. "Nah, you just needed me."

Titus peeked out of one eye as his heartbeat accelerated. What did Draven mean by that? Did he think Titus was becoming emotionally involved? That he would think this was more than it truly was? Did he — ?

Draven pressed his hips to Titus'. The hot, thick length of his cock short-circuited Titus' panicking brain.

"Oh yeah, need you," he rasped.

Before Titus could do anything else, blurt out something embarrassing, Draven kissed him, deep and dirty, no gentle nips and licks.

Titus moaned, opened his mouth and lost himself in the taste of Draven, the feel of his body, the scent of the ocean rolling off him. There was *nothing* about Draven that didn't flip every one of Titus' switches.

Titus ran his hands up from the mounds of Draven's ass to his face. He kissed Draven back with every ounce of enthusiasm he had, without inhibition, reveling in the moment rather than worrying about in it.

He pressed his head against the pillow to give himself a little space because he needed to speak. "Wanna suck you."

Draven rumbled and kissed him again, then Draven was pushing up, moving while Titus caressed his thighs, his abs, his chest.

Draven grabbed his pillow. "Raise up."

Titus lifted his head and let Draven shove the pillow under him.

"Perfect," Draven murmured. "Open for me. Show me you want it."

Titus burned with need as he parted his lips. He'd never known how much he liked dirty talk, maybe because he'd never been with anyone who had done it right.

Draven did everything right.

Including feeding the tip of his cock into Titus' mouth so slowly that Titus was in danger of drooling on himself, his mouth was watering so much. He wanted to taste Draven, and when he flicked his tongue over Draven's slit, the briny taste reminded him of the ocean.

Titus sucked on the tip, and Draven hissed. "Can I…?" He slipped one hand around to the back of Titus' head. "Is this okay?"

"Mmhm." Titus cupped Draven's ass. He ran his tongue around the top then the underside of Draven's crown.

Draven cursed softly and jerked, pushing deeper into Titus' mouth.

Titus sealed his lips around Draven's length and used his tongue to tease along the shaft. He wanted more. He sucked and tried to raise his head.

"Hungry for it," Draven muttered, then pressed in, oh so slowly, until he breached Titus' throat.

Titus swallowed and relished the sound Draven made—he was every bit as hungry for this as Titus was.

"Sweet hell," Draven whispered. "You're going to kill me."

Titus hoped not. He wanted those promised days with Draven.

Draven rolled his hips, his taut butt clenching and releasing under Titus' hands. He took Draven's cock into his throat again, and Draven shivered.

"N-not—" Draven pulled back. "Not y-yet."

Titus was confused—*who didn't want a blow job?*— until Draven turned around and pushed Titus' legs apart.

Fuck yes! Titus drew Draven's cock back into his mouth as Draven fisted his shaft in return.

Titus cupped Draven's balls with one hand and kneaded his ass with the other.

Draven lapped at Titus' glans, murmuring and moaning, then bobbed down, sucking most of Titus' length into the hot, wet cavern of his mouth.

Titus cried out around Draven's cock. Electric sparks of pleasure were shooting along his nerve endings – he wasn't going to last long.

He tried to concentrate on driving Draven out of his mind, swallowing every chance he could, pressing and rolling Draven's sac, working the fingers of his other hand into Draven's crease to tease at his hole.

That last bit seemed to rock Draven's world. His hips stuttered and his thrusting turned rougher, wilder.

Titus sucked harder and his balls drew tight when Draven pushed a finger against his hole. He hadn't even penetrated Titus before Titus' orgasm slammed into him with the force of a tsunami.

He was dimly aware of Draven shouting, of the swell of Draven's prick and the taste of his cum. It was hard to do anything but believe he'd morphed into a being made entirely of ecstasy as he came.

Titus was panting as Draven flopped to the side, his feet by Titus' head. Every few seconds, he felt Draven shudder, heard his raspy breaths between Titus'.

Titus knew he should do something, say something.

"Swim," Draven said, his voice rough, likely from taking Titus' dick deep down his throat.

Titus was on the verge of passing out into a sex-stupor. "Uh?"

"Swim. I need –" Draven cleared his throat, not that his voice sounded any better when he spoke again. "Water. Get in the water."

Titus frowned, then shrugged. He knew Draven loved the ocean. It didn't really surprise him that Draven would want a middle-of-the-night swim. Maybe it should have.

This was the only vacation fling Titus would ever have, though. He wasn't the kind of person who did this type of thing, so he was going to enjoy every second of it.

"Come with me?" Draven asked, sitting up and holding out his hand.

Titus took a hold of it. "Yeah." He'd been ready to pass out, but the idea of spending some time playing in the ocean with Draven was too appealing to pass up. "Let's go."

Chapter Ten

Three nights left

Three nights — that wasn't much time.

"Hey, here comes the dolphin again." Titus chuckled. "It sure seems to like you."

Draven was going to have a chat with the aquarium's dolphin, Kai. If Kai kept approaching Draven, someone was bound to notice — Kai's trainers, for example.

"I think he's eyeing you," Draven said as he silently willed Kai to behave. *Everyone thinks dolphins are sweet creatures. Little do they know...*

Titus looked from Kai to Draven, then back at Kai. "No, no he's definitely wanting your attention. Maybe we should walk around to the surface level."

"I have a better idea. Let's go see the otters." In truth, Draven hated coming to the aquarium, but Titus had wanted to go, and he'd talked about how he could use the experience for some of his lesson plans. It gave

Draven the creeps to see all the creatures in captivity. *Only for Titus would I do this.*

Titus pressed his hand to the thick glass of the underground viewing area. "Look, here comes the other dolphin."

"Mmhm. Otters are really cute." Two dolphins vying for Draven's attention—or trying to cause trouble for him, more likely—could only spell trouble. "And there's ice cream to be had."

Titus looked at him. "Do you have a fear of dolphins?"

A justified one. "Some people call them the bullies of the sea."

"What?" Titus frowned. "No! Everyone knows dolphins are good…things…aren't they?"

Guilt settled like a knot in Draven's gut. "I didn't mean to ruin your fun."

Titus' frown gave way to a smile. "You didn't. I won't be passing on the bad news about dolphins to my new students. I've been trying to get the school to let us bring the kids here for the last field trip of the school year, but I always get shot down. Think maybe the admins know about the evil of dolphins?"

Since Titus was teasing, the lump of guilt began to dissipate. "It's highly possible. Word's been getting out about dolphins trying to take over the world. Them and the octopuses."

"Octopuses." Titus shivered as they began walking out of the viewing area. "Man, I know those things are really smart. I've seen videos of them escaping from aquariums and moving on dry land. One of my college roommates had a theory that octopuses were actually aliens. I don't know why he thought that. I never asked, but every time I see an octopus on TV or online, I get creeped out."

"They're very smart, but they aren't evil." *Like some dolphins I know.* "That's my opinion, anyway," Draven rushed to add before Titus thought he was weird. They stepped out into the humid Texas day. The air felt thicker but familiar. The salty tang in it made Draven's skin hum with an almost electric-current sensation.

"Do you ever wonder if it's wrong to keep animals in captivity?" Titus asked. "We take the kids to the zoo for their first field trip, and I always feel bad for most of the animals. Kind of having the same experience here."

"I don't like to see anything caged," Draven admitted with honesty before he could think better of it.

Titus turned to him and stopped walking. "Then why are we here? You should have spoken up."

Draven shrugged. "You wanted to come here. That's what mattered more to me."

"It mattered more than your own feelings?" Titus asked quietly as he studied Draven.

Draven's cheeks heated with a blush. How did he dare answer that?

Titus saved him from having to stress over it. "Let's go."

"Wait. I didn't mean to ruin this for you." Draven felt like an ass. "Ignore what I said. Let's go see the otters."

Titus shook his head. "I'm not going to ignore what you said. What you want is…is important to me, too."

This is just a fling. Just a fling. Three nights left.

"Draven?" Titus touched his arm.

It's just a fling, but it's going to hurt like a motherfucker when he leaves. Draven plastered on a smile. "Sorry, I was thinking about what else we can do."

Titus leaned in and whispered, "You can take me back to your place and fuck me stupid. If that's what you want. I *know* I'll love it."

Draven's heart beat faster and blood rushed down to his groin. "Are you sure?"

Titus had moved back, and he rolled his eyes. "Oh my gosh. How could I prefer this" — he waved a hand around him — "over what I proposed?"

Draven's smile was much sincere this time. "Well, if you're absolutely sure…?"

"Unless you'd rather be here?" Titus asked. "I know what I'd pick, but hey —"

Draven caught Titus by an elbow. "Home it is."

Titus laughed and a few people looked their way. Draven had never touched another man out in public, not in any way that wasn't familial, but with the promise of having his cock buried in Titus' tight ass soon, Draven was unable to keep from touching him. And it was only a hand to Titus' elbow. If someone wanted to cause trouble because of it, Draven would slap the daylights out of them.

No one bothered them as they left the aquarium and walked back to Titus' car. The anticipation was taut between them. If there hadn't been people lulling about, Draven would have spoken, would have told Titus all the dirty things he was going to do to him when they got to Draven's place.

"Hurry," Draven muttered once they were in the car. "Gods, I want to kiss you so bad right now."

Titus stopped mid-buckling up. "Do it. I want —"

Draven swallowed the rest of those words, the whimpers and moans Titus gave him, too. He didn't worry about being seen or someone causing trouble.

All he could think about was Titus, and some little voice in his head told him that was going to cause him trouble enough.

Draven ignored it. This was just a fling. His heart couldn't possibly be at risk.

Chapter Eleven

Two nights left

The moonlight was partially obscured by clouds, but it didn't dim the romance of the night. Titus relished holding Draven's hand in his, the wet sand under their feet, the breeze blowing with a tad more gusto than usual, the salt in the air. Although the night itself was nearly perfect, it was the man walking with him that held his attention.

Draven stopped them and pointed at a pier. "I was actually under there when I first saw you."

It didn't even seem odd to Titus. Draven was...different, and though Titus couldn't pinpoint how, he wasn't bothered by it. "When Riveen came out of the water?"

"Yes." Draven walked them to the edge of where the waves could lap at their feet. "We swim a lot. The ocean is...necessary. I couldn't imagine living away from the ocean. I couldn't live away from it."

Titus thought Draven was being melodramatic, but he got the message loud and clear—Titus wasn't creating fluffy dreams of Draven moving back with him. Besides, Draven wouldn't be who he was without having the ocean nearby. Titus ignored the little pain in his heart. *This is just a fling, and it'll be over soon.*

"Are you up to a swim?" Draven asked. He grinned at Titus. "I'll keep you safe."

Titus laughed. "Maybe *I'll* keep *you* safe."

Draven surprised Titus by pulling him in for a kiss. Titus opened immediately, running his hands down to Draven's butt. He kneaded the taut mounds and tilted his head to deepen the kiss.

Draven rumbled and cupped him at the nape and jaw. Titus felt the growing bulge of Draven's erection, the answering swell of his own.

"Not much time left," Draven murmured against Titus' lips.

Titus didn't want to think about that. He kissed Draven again and explored the many flavors of him. Draven always tasted slightly salty. It was a part of him that fascinated Titus, that he was coming to crave.

No, no craving. No craving. He nipped Draven's tongue and moved his hands so that he could run his fingers down Draven's crease.

Water splashed over their feet as Titus—and Draven—sank into the sand with each wave. Draven tugged, and they moved a few steps into the ocean.

Titus had learned to leave his cell phone and wallet at the condo unless he knew they were going out somewhere he'd need it. Draven liked his spontaneous dips in the ocean, and Titus was learning to appreciate them, too.

Especially when Draven made a growling sort of noise before taking them a little deeper into the warm ocean.

Titus kept his hands on Draven, kept tracing the seam of his ass through the thin swim trunks he wore for Titus' sake. Then he felt the water lapping at his thighs and a surge of daring had him pulling Draven's trunks down.

And still they kissed, Draven's breath hitching when Titus bared his cock. Draven moaned softly and licked at Titus' lips.

Titus had to stop touching Draven long enough to jerk his own shorts down. His cock bobbed in the water, and Draven pressed up against him. Titus went right back to playing with Draven's ass, tracing the slightly fuzzy length of his crack. He tapped Draven's hole and Draven jolted, thrusting his hips demandingly.

Titus took them another step out, then another, and the water covered most of their asses. He nipped Draven's lip then pressed a fingertip against Draven's pucker.

Draven made his rumbling sound again as he shot a hand down to grab Titus' butt. Without hesitation, he pushed a thick finger into Titus' hole.

Titus went hot all over, inside and out. His legs trembled but he had enough brain cells still working to keep in the game. He ran his fingertip around Draven's ring, teasing as Draven growled and began fucking him with just the one finger.

That lit Titus up and made his balls tingle with the threat of orgasm. They drew up tight in a matter of seconds, and Titus turned his head, gasping for breath.

Draven rocked his hips, and Titus pushed his finger into the tight heat of Draven's body. Draven let out a soft curse, then demanded, "More!"

"No lube," Titus muttered, opening his eyes only to discover everything was blurry. He shuddered when Draven nibbled at his neck. "Fuck."

Draven began sucking up a mark, and Titus grunted as he got his finger moving again, pushing in, slipping out, then in again to work it in a circle, stretching Draven's rim.

"Yes," Draven hissed before biting Titus just hard enough to sting in the way he loved. "Need more."

Titus would have asked what Draven meant, but he was beyond words. Then Draven was pulling away.

"What—?" Titus began.

Draven pointed to the pier. "Getting a condom. Want you to fuck me under there."

Titus blinked until he could see decently. "You want…?"

Draven nodded. "Where I first saw you, yes."

Titus swallowed around a lump in his throat. That sounded romantic, caring—not like casual affair at all.

Still, he nodded and watched as Draven took a condom from his pocket along with a packet of lube. "Least they didn't float off."

"Yeah."

Draven moved to the shallower water, and Titus followed. They both kicked their shorts up onto dry ground, then Draven grinned at him, looking so young and happy that Titus went dizzy.

Not because he was sick, or off balance.

But because he knew he'd done something really stupid.

He refused to think about it as Draven took his hand and placed the packets in it. "Come fuck me." Draven sprinted through the shallow water, toward the pier.

"No thinking," Titus whispered, then chased after Draven.

Draven was too quick to catch. Even when the water was knee-deep, he moved like he was a part of it.

Titus stumbled a time or two, but he wasn't far behind Draven.

Draven stopped under the pier and planted his hands against one of the posts. The water was still knee-deep, and Titus glanced around to make sure no one was on the beach.

"We're under the pier, in the shadows. No one will see us," Draven said. "Fuck me, Titus." He spread his legs and arched his back. "I need you in me, now."

Titus closed the distance between them. "You'll have me in you, but first—" He pressed Draven's cheeks apart, one hand still clutching the supplies. "First, this."

Draven looked back over his shoulder. "This what?" Then he sucked in a sharp breath as Titus licked a path down his crease. "Oh! No one ever... No one... I—" He made a choked sound when Titus lapped at his hole.

Titus was glad no one else had ever rimmed Draven. He wanted to be the first, the last—*No, no, no!*

Titus closed his eyes and laved Draven's hole, loosening up the muscles and soaking them until they were slick, and he could slip his tongue inside.

Draven made another choked sound, then began to pant as Titus tongued him.

Titus pressed and squeezed Draven's ass, licked down to his balls then back to his hole, giving Draven all he had. Every sound Draven made, every movement, the feel of his skin, the clench of his body, the taste and scent of him — it was all seared into Titus' soul. He'd remember it, each second, for the rest of his life.

He tried to deny those thoughts, and ones like them, but they wouldn't cease. Titus gave in and gave of himself, putting every bit of the emotions he wouldn't speak into his actions.

When Draven begged him to fuck him, Titus gave Draven's hole one last lick, then kissed his way up to Draven's lower back. Titus opened the condom as he nibbled there, and with shaking he hands, managed to get the condom on.

"Hurry," Draven mumbled, his hips moving as if Titus were already in him.

"I am." Titus opened the lube packet. He slicked his cock, rubbed the remaining lube over Draven's hole, then lined up his shaft with one hand. In the other, he gripped the empty packages — neither he nor Draven took kindly to littering in the ocean, and even the heavy weight of lust and need wouldn't make Titus forget that.

He slowly pushed against Draven's pucker. "You're so tight."

Draven grunted and startled Titus by pushing back, hard.

That made them both yelp.

"Draven, don't —" *hurt yourself.* The rest of Titus' words were drowned out by Draven's demand that he keep going.

Titus wanted to ask if Draven was sure, but he wouldn't have appreciated the second-guessing were he in Draven's shoes. Titus slid both arms around Draven and thrust, probably gentler than Draven would have wanted, but he was just too tight to plow right into.

"Ungh, m-more," Draven rasped. "Gimme more!"

Titus rested his head against Draven's back and made small movements, penetrating deeper and deeper with each one.

Draven alternately cursed and squirmed, canting his hips.

Titus knew what it felt like to need to be fucked. He tightened his hold on Draven, and gave him more, sharper, quicker thrusts until he had his cock thoroughly buried in Draven's ass.

Draven hissed and swiveled his hips, clenching and releasing around Titus' cock.

"Holy— Don't do that if you want this to last more than a few seconds," Titus whispered. "You feel incredible. So tight."

"Can't handle it?" Draven clenched again. "Fuck me!"

Titus gave up trying to be noble. Draven knew what he wanted.

Titus let go of Draven long enough to grip his hips, then pulled almost all the way out before thrusting in again powerfully enough to drive a grunt out of Draven.

"Like that," Draven said huskily. "Harder!"

Titus didn't hold back. He withdrew most of the way then drove back in, harder and harder every time.

Draven cursed. He grunted. He whimpered and begged for more.

Titus grabbed his shoulders and gave it to him. He couldn't pull back as much but he could slam in with increased force.

Draven keened and braced one forearm on the post. His other arm began moving as he jacked himself off. His ass gripped Titus' cock tighter, and Titus' balls drew up. He gritted his teeth and prayed that Draven came first.

And Draven did, throwing his head back and shouting, his entire body shaking. Titus' control broke and he slammed in once, twice, then froze as his orgasm ripped through him, leaving chaos and bliss in its wake.

Titus was dimly aware of reaching down and making sure he didn't lose the condom as Draven moved, then Draven was facing him, holding him, comforting him. Titus didn't know why his heart hurt. It didn't make sense, and as he leaned against Draven, he dashed tears from his eyes before Draven could see them.

Chapter Twelve

One night left

"Seriously, bro? You let him fuck you against a barnacle-covered post?"

Draven groaned and splashed Riveen. "Shut up, you pervert. Why were you even watching?"

Riveen had easily dodged the spray. He rolled his eyes at Draven. "Right, blame *me* when I was just out for a swim! You *know* that's part of our territory. And you've been spending all your time with Titus, so I was maybe feeling sorry for myself and lonely."

Guilt settled on Draven's shoulders and pressed against his chest. "Riv, I'm sorry, but it's only — for one more day." *Geez, his chest hurt.* "You can't blame me for wanting to spend all the time with him that I can."

Riv sniffed and floated a few feet back. "I can, too. If I'd known you'd be too busy for me, maybe I wouldn't have set you two up. Where is lover-boy today?"

Draven barely resisted the impulse to glance in the direction of Titus' condo. He couldn't see it from here, but it wasn't far away. "He's taking a nap."

Riveen stopped floating and leered at him. "Oh-ho! You wore him out! Or, I mean, he wore you out, except that doesn't work even though I saw him fucking you into the nasty beam."

"Riv, can you stop talking about that?" Draven shuddered. "It's fucking disturbing."

Riveen bobbed his head. "You're telling me! I was just swimming along, stirring the sand here and there and chasing seaweed, then I saw — that." Riveen shuddered. "Believe it or not, I didn't hang around and keep watching. I think it's only fair that I be allowed to give you shit for exposing me to such a brain-scarring sight."

Draven looked up at the sky and sighed. "Fine. I'm sorry I scarred you for life. *Now* can we stop talking about it?"

Riveen grinned. "Definitely. So was that the first time you bottomed?"

"Riv," Draven growled, ready to throttle him.

Riveen squealed, dove under water and shifted.

Draven hesitated for half a second — long enough to make sure no one was around — then he dove under the water and shifted as well.

Riveen was smaller and faster, but Draven's wingspan was greater. He could catch Riveen in a race of distance, if not of speed.

The water caressed him, almost like a full-body massage as he swam. Draven relished the freedom he had in this form. Riveen dipped and spun around ahead of him, then made a wide turn and circled Draven.

Draven flipped over—he'd had Riveen nip him more than once.

Riveen zigged and zagged—

—and Draven, who had been so serious for so long, wanted suddenly to play.

What'll it hurt? I've been caretaker for our kind for so long... Just a little fun. That's all I want right now.

Like I want Titus.

But Draven wanted Titus for more than 'right now'.

He shut off the threat of the depressing reality there, and instead flapped one wing at Riveen.

Riveen stilled, and his little eyes widened. His mouth moved and he sank to the bottom.

Draven would have laughed—he'd shocked his brother something good—but instead of laughing, Draven slapped the sandy bottom and sent up a cloud that obscured his view.

It also obscured Riveen's, which Draven took advantage of, shooting off as fast as he could through the water.

Sunlight penetrated the warm sanctuary. It was beautiful, the water clear—except behind him—and the sun streaming bright through to the ocean floor.

A few jellyfish tried to keep up with him, but Draven was too fast for them. He zipped toward the pier.

He could feel Riveen coming up behind him, sense the change in the water and the pressure, hear his movements. Draven tried to swim faster, but Riveen shot past him and made sure to swat sand in his face.

It was fun. Draven felt years drop away, worries and fears eclipsed by a moment of joy, a memory in the making that he'd treasure forever.

He was going to lose Titus. He knew that. There was no way for them to remain together.

So he needed to remember this, too — the bright sun, the warm water, the happiness and freedom of his body slicing through the waves.

He'd need all the good memories he could store up, because, once Titus left, Draven knew he'd hurt and ache for the man.

Chapter Thirteen

Out of time

Titus dreamed of waves, of warm water and squishy sand, the brush of seaweed against his ankle, the salty tang in the air, the stroke of sunlight on his skin.

He didn't want to wake up, didn't want reality to pull him from that blissful world he was in.

Then reality became better than the dream as a warm, hard body pressed against him. Titus sighed and spread his legs, allowing Draven to settle between them.

Titus knew Draven's scent, the feel of him, the weight of his body, the length of his cock.

That cock was aligned with his, slick and perfect. Some dim part of Titus' brain wondered how Draven had been awake enough to think of lube, but Draven began sucking on that spot under Titus' ear and thoughts ceased to be a thing.

All there was in the world then was feeling, sensations, skin on skin and bodies pressing together.

Titus caressed every inch of Draven he could reach and opened his eyes to find Draven staring intently at him, not even blinking as he rubbed off with Titus.

Titus wrapped his legs around Draven's and thrust up. Heat coiled in his groin. He could hardly draw in a breath when Draven's cockhead caught the underside of his. Titus jolted and moaned, arching his neck, his back. "More," he forced out past his dry lips. "Gimme more."

Draven bit him, scraping his teeth over the spot he'd sucked on. Titus shivered. "Please, Draven, please!"

Draven nudged his lips. "Please what?"

Titus growled. "Fuck me!"

"Yes. Gonna fuck you so good you won't be able to forget me."

Titus tried to make sense of those words. He couldn't, not when he already knew he'd never forget Draven.

Draven grabbed a package off the nightstand, ripped it open and rolled on the condom — all in a matter of seconds.

Titus clutched at his arm when Draven would have picked up the lube and shook his head. "Let me."

"Jesus," Draven muttered. He sat back on his heels after Titus let go of him.

Titus wasn't prone to displaying himself like he was about to, but...*but this is Draven. He can see all of me. I don't want to hide.* Titus snatched up the lube and flipped the cap. He coated two fingers and handed the bottle to Draven to deal with.

Titus raised his legs so his knees were almost touching his chest. He watched Draven's gaze follow the movement of his hand as he reached down to rub his slick fingers over his hole.

"Fuck," Draven rasped. "Put 'em in."

"Not yet." Titus teased his pucker, pressing, massaging, but not penetrating it. He played with one nipple and his vision clouded as pleasure built inside him. He started to press his fingers into his ass but stopped. He knew what he wanted.

"C'mere." He held his hand out to Draven. "Let me slick you up."

"You should —"

"I want *you*," Titus said, making sure he spoke with a firm tone. "You, not my fingers. Just go slow at first."

Draven nodded and scooted closer. Titus used the lube left on his fingers to coat Draven's cock.

"Now."

Draven hooked one arm under Titus' left leg and lined his cock up to Titus' hole. "You'll tell me if it hurts."

It wasn't a question, but Titus still said, "Yes."

Draven bent down to kiss him, a press of lips and melding of tongues that left Titus lightheaded. Draven raised his head an inch or so, his lips hovering just above Titus'. The press of Draven's crown to Titus' hole sent a shiver throughout Titus.

Titus gripped Draven's shoulders and let his eyes roll back and close as Draven's cockhead began to breach him. The burn was exquisite, and Titus wanted it, wanted to feel Draven's presence there for as long as he could.

Draven's breath hitched as the glans slipped in. "Titus," he whispered.

Titus forced his eyes open, couldn't look away while Draven slowly filled him.

When Draven bottomed out, he took another kiss, gentle at first. Titus clenched around him, working

Draven's cock with his internal walls. The kiss went from tender to rough, a crush of lips as Draven began to move, canting his hips before he slammed back in.

He dropped to his elbows and grabbed handfuls of Titus' hair. Draven kissed Titus as fiercely as he fucked him, and Titus reveled in the mix of pleasure and pain, in knowing Draven's control was as shot as his own. He curled his fingers against Draven's biceps, let his nails scrape, wound his legs around Draven's hips and prodded him with his heels.

Every time Draven withdrew, Titus jerked him in again. Draven growled and bit at his lips, fucking him harder and harder still.

Titus was on fire, and he wasn't sure it was an orgasm he had to have. Something was growing in him, something huge and hungry and needy.

He tried to suppress it. Feelings like those weren't allowed. His whimpers were as much from pleasure as from fear that he'd say words he absolutely shouldn't speak.

Draven powered into him faster, hammering his hips against Titus' ass. Every time his abs rubbed over Titus' dick, pleasure shot down to Titus' balls.

Titus tried to keep his focus on that, on the physical pleasure, but the emotions he wanted to ignore raged inside him.

He turned his head aside and bit his wrist, trying desperately to stop himself from speaking.

Draven nipped his jaw, his ear, then rose enough to fist Titus' shaft.

Titus screamed as his orgasm tore through him, demolishing words and breath and *everything* in stunning waves of bliss. He heard Draven call out his name, felt him stiffen, buck his hips.

Then he saw Draven clearly—the pleasure making his face glow as he climaxed.

And he saw something else, something in Draven's gaze that looked like the unspoken words Titus had somehow held back.

But neither of them spoke those words. Theirs was a week-long fling.

It was too bad Titus' heart refused to believe that.

Chapter Fourteen

Draven tossed down another shot of tequila then leaned his head back and stared up at the ceiling. It was starting to spin, which wasn't a surprise. He had a low tolerance for alcohol, and, as exhausted as he was, that tolerance had to be almost non-existent.

He had a feeling that all the booze in the world wouldn't help him do what he was trying to do. Oh, not forget Titus — he knew that wasn't going to happen. But he'd hoped to take the edge off the sharp pain of loss that had remained with him since Titus had left.

"You must be shitfaced if you didn't even hear me come in."

Draven hadn't heard Riveen, and he was too drunk and too tired to even be startled. He closed his eyes as the ceiling spun a little faster. "Whatever." And either he slurred the word, or his hearing was messed up.

"Tequila?" Riveen snorted. "Gods, you really want to make yourself miserable, huh?"

"M'already misherable." Yeah, his ears were screwed up. Or his tongue. "Thongue."

"Aaannnnd that's enough for you."

Draven raised his head, opened his eyes and somehow managed only to yelp a little when the entire world dipped. He'd have sworn his chair moved, which was why his ass hit the floor. "Ow!"

"You're such a wuss." Riveen was squatting by him. "And you hate getting drunk. Did Titus really get to you?"

Draven cradled his head in his hands, trying to keep whatever it was from swirling.

"I know you swam up the coastline for miles. Were you following his car?"

Draven started to nod, thought better of it, and grunted, "Nyeah."

"Oh damn it." Riveen sighed and ran a hand over Draven's hair. "You tender-hearted idiot. You *knew* he was leaving, and after —"

"No!" Draven would never be so drunk that he'd want to go *there*. He refused to even think *That One's* name.

"Drav, it's been years— Never mind," Riveen muttered. "No reasoning with a drunk. Let me get you some water."

The ocean sounded like a good place to be. Draven tried to get up but quickly realized he needed to hold himself stationary since everything else was moving. "Schwim."

"Jeez, dude, not when you can't even talk right. Do *not* move."

Draven closed his eyes but that was worse than having them open. "Fuuuuck."

"Yeah, you'll be saying that a lot in the morning. You know tequila turns you inside out. You must really like Titus."

'Like' was too mild a word, but Draven wisely kept his mouth shut.

Just like I kept it shut around Titus. Didn't tell him. Guess it doesn't matter. He left. He left me.

"If you're gonna be a sappy drunk, I'm giving you a few more shots of tequila so you'll just pass out for twelve hours."

Draven flipped Riveen off...maybe. He might not have gotten the right finger up or used too many of them.

"Shit!" he bellowed when Riveen doused him with iced water.

"There. That oughta help you sober up."

"You ashhole!" Draven tried to kick at Riveen, who apparently had gotten a freakin' five-gallon barrel of iced water. It just kept coming and coming.

Then it wasn't, and Draven was in the bathroom, and Riveen was shoving him in the shower, clothes and all.

Draven had no idea how he'd gotten from the living room floor to where he was. He was lucky he didn't drown himself in the shower as the hot water pelted him.

"Dunno if that's the right way to sober up someone who's drunk," Riveen was saying. "But I did enjoy dumping the pitcher of water on you."

"Pitcher?" Draven blinked and swiped at the water running into his eyes. It dawned on him to move his head out from under the direct line of spray.

"Yeah, pitcher. You know, the one you keep in the fridge?" Riveen handed him something.

Draven took it. It was a toothbrush.

"Use it, bro. You have gut-rot breath. Like something you ate crawled back up and festered in your mouth."

"Urk." Draven slapped a hand over his mouth. It'd have been nice if he'd remembered he had the toothbrush in that hand. He jabbed himself in the eye. "Fuck!" The burn caused by the toothpaste made him whimper.

"You are a fucking menace to yourself!" Riveen yanked the toothbrush out of his hand. "Gods, I better get a brother of the year award for this."

Then Riveen was in the shower with him, also clothed, although Draven thought he only had on swim trunks.

"Come on. Get out of these."

It was easier to let Riveen undress him than to fight about it. Draven stumbled a few times and smacked his head once against the tiled wall. Other than that, he was relatively unscathed when Riveen handed him a body scrubber.

Draven washed himself automatically. His arms ached — all his body ached from swimming so far and fast.

"Soons he lefth, I ran out —" he began.

Riveen coughed. "Let me, er, let me get that toothbrush back in here. I can help you use it."

"Can do it myself," Draven snapped as his head began to pound. "Oh fuck. My head."

Riveen didn't comment, just handed him the toothbrush once more. "If this is about Titus leaving, aren't you being a tad melodramatic?"

Draven shoved the toothbrush in his mouth and glared at Riveen.

Riveen rolled his eyes. "Please, like I'm scared of you. Nope. You have Titus' phone number, right?"

Of *course* he did. They'd texted every day, making plans or just chatting.

"And he doesn't live that far away. Less than two hours. That's not even far enough apart to qualify as a long-distance relationship if you want to keep seeing him."

Riveen needed to quit making sense.

Draven spoke around the toothbrush. "He left."

Riveen gave him another eye-roll. "Would that be *after* you asked him if you could keep seeing each other?"

"I didn't ask him." *Oops.* Draven had drunkenly stumbled right into that one.

"Right, you didn't ask him about it, because this way, you could be all wounded and not risk your heart," Riveen said. "Like you did with Arin."

Draven jerked the toothbrush from his mouth and pointed it at Riveen. "Don't go there! You don't know what it's like to have your heart broken!"

Riveen nodded. "True. I'm not interested in that organ. I prefer to focus on the one lower down." He grabbed his crotch. "Keeps me from ending up drunk as shit in a shower."

"You're still in a shower *with* a drunk," Draven retorted.

"Oh good! You're surly again. You must be sobering up." Riveen adjusted the showerhead so that the water smacked Draven right in the face. "Finish up in here and put an end to your pity party. Don't lie to me and, more importantly, don't lie to yourself. You didn't want Titus enough to take a risk on him, so you don't deserve to feel abandoned. You could have talked to him."

"He could have talked to me," Draven argued. He started brushing his teeth again.

"What if he was hurt? Did you ever think about that?" Riveen asked. "How much do you know about Titus' past? Maybe he has reasons to be afraid to take a risk on you. Maybe it wasn't a case of him not wanting you but being too afraid. Like you. Geez, I'm thinking you're both idiots. I bet he got attached to you. He didn't strike me as the casual sort, which is why I didn't really try to get in his pants."

Draven stared at his brother, too stunned by Riveen's insight to even inform him that Titus would have *never* hooked up with him. Was Riveen right? Draven recalled the awkwardness between him and Titus before they'd parted, the way Titus wouldn't look directly at him. *Titus' hands were trembling when he'd tried to lock the condo door. He dropped the keys twice. His breathing was funny. Why didn't I ask him what was wrong?*

But Draven knew the answer. He hadn't asked because he hadn't wanted to see, hadn't wanted to know. "Damn it."

"What?" Riveen asked before laughing. "Oh, I know. You realized I'm right and you've been a jerk."

Draven would get Riveen a brother of the year award, and smack him with it.

Chapter Fifteen

Summer was going to drag by. Titus wished he'd been able to teach summer school—he'd have had something to help pass the time. As it was, he'd spent the week since he'd returned from the coast moping around like a lovesick fool. And he'd put off dinner with Stacy and Michelle. If he told them that he was ill a second time, they'd show up at his doorstep.

The idea of spending an evening with them made his heart ache, and it also made him feel like the biggest asshole in the world, because he was envious of their relationship. He wanted that kind of bond...and he knew who he wanted it with.

"Stupid. Don't be stupid." Titus opened his eyes and gave the bridge of his nose a rest. He got up from the couch and stretched. Maybe he'd feel less moody if he actually left the house.

That meant showering first. Titus sniffed his pits. "Definitely showering."

There was no point in sitting around feeling sorry for himself, or thinking he was heartbroken. That last one was stupid. He and Draven hadn't even spent a full week together. It wasn't like Titus loved him. That just wasn't possible in such a short time.

I'm going to stop thinking about him. Just stop it, Titus. Stop the pity party and pouting and all the other crappy p-words that are downers. If he gave himself that lecture often enough, eventually it'd actually sink in.

Just like if he kept telling himself there was no way he could have truly fallen for Draven. It was only the sex, and the fact that Titus hadn't had any involving someone other than himself in years.

And the reason for *that* didn't bear thinking about. There was nothing Titus could do to change the past.

But I could stop letting it control my future.

Titus groaned and stripped off his clothes in the bathroom. He wasn't in the mood for any deep thinking. He was just in a summer funk. That was *all* that was wrong with him.

He should be reveling in the adventure he'd had. *Think about the good times, the sex, Draven…*

"Fuck. Ugh!" Titus stepped into the shower and turned it on. The water was cold, but Texas was hot, and Titus hadn't bumped the AC down, so he was fine being pelted by chilled water.

He cleaned himself almost mechanically until he reached the lower part of his stomach. Then parts started tingling and images burst into his head like they'd been held back by a bungee cord that had snapped.

Draven, kissing him, touching him, fucking him—and Draven smiling, scowling, laughing, leaning close to whisper in his ear, sharing touristy info and sexual innuendos.

And rather than becoming aroused, Titus' mood plummeted. He missed Draven. Lying to himself about it wasn't helping. Whether it was stupid or not, he missed the man.

That might have only been the case because Titus had been alone for so long. Not that he'd had options where he lived…the dating pool for him was borderline microscopic, and even Stacy and Michelle kept their relationship hidden.

Titus didn't want to live like that, not if he found someone he loved.

But he hadn't found that someone yet.

Yes, you have.

"Shut up," Titus muttered to the voice in his head. "I have not!"

He finished cleaning up then turned the shower off. He hadn't stopped thinking about Draven, but he was going to try to stop being so down about their fling coming to an end. They'd both agreed on what they'd done beforehand. Titus'd had no right to change the established rules even though he'd wanted to ask Draven if there was a way to make a relationship work. Although Titus wasn't sure he'd have actually been brave enough to speak up.

He walked into his bedroom, a towel around his hips. His phone screen was lit up, so he'd either had a missed call or a text. Or both.

Titus was betting on a text from Stacy. He really needed to get over himself and go see her and Michelle. Maybe he'd call her and offer to show up with pizza for dinner tomorrow. They could watch a movie and stuff themselves on cheesy, greasy goodness.

That was what he'd do. Titus crossed over to his phone before he could change his mind. The screen went dark just before he got there, but he picked up his phone then tapped it.

And almost dropped it when he saw the text.

Can I come talk to you?

Titus' heart pounded so hard he halfway expected to keel over. He placed a hand on his chest as he reread the message from Draven. He hadn't been able to delete Draven's contact info, but even if he had, he would have known that number.

And though it was possible that he should have given the request some thought, Titus didn't. He replied with,

Yes, of course. Would love to see you again.

It was perhaps too enthusiastic, but it was still less than what Titus held back.

Draven answered him in seconds.

I'm at the Holiday Inn. Be there in five minutes.

"Here?" Titus squeaked. "He's already here?"

Is that okay?

Draven texted.

Titus nodded then groaned because Draven couldn't see him bobbing his head. He answered just as quickly with,

More than okay.

Now all Titus needed to do was to decide on whether to open the door while wearing the towel, or while wearing nothing at all.

Because he wanted Draven, and yes, he wanted to talk to him, but first...

Yeah, but first —

Chapter Sixteen

It was hard to breathe so far away from the ocean. Draven splashed water on his face then looked at his reflection in the mirror. The hotel's lighting made his skin look pasty — at least, he hoped it was the lighting. The water didn't refresh him as much as the ocean would have, but it helped some. If he was going to be spending weekends or whatever there, he might start bringing a few gallons of saltwater with him.

Draven toweled off his face then ran his fingers through his hair. He was damned nervous, though judging by Titus' speedy reply, he wanted to see Draven. Surely that meant Titus would be open to a relationship.

Draven only shivered a little as he turned away from the mirror. He left the hotel room then had to go back in to get the condoms and packets of lube. He was being optimistic, true, but he and Titus had burned up the sheets most of the times they were together, barring when they were in public places.

And the pier...

Draven's cock began to harden. He ignored that horny beast and drove to Titus' house. Draven had scoped it out earlier. Small, brick, clean yard — and Titus inside, that was all Draven cared to notice.

He parked then unbuckled and got out. The heat made his skin burn and sweat break out on his brow. Draven decided not to worry about it. He and Titus had been sweaty together much of the time back at home.

Draven patted his shirt pocket, where the condoms and lube were weighing it down. He removed them and put them in the back pocket of his jeans.

He closed the distance between him and Titus' front door. Anxiety and anticipation were battling for dominance in him. Draven knocked and hoped it was okay to be optimistic. He might end up being rejected —

The door opened then Titus was *right there*, and one of them moved, or both of them, Draven couldn't have said, and it didn't matter. He had Titus in his arms, was crushing his mouth to Titus' and backing him inside. Draven kicked the door shut and spun Titus, pressing him against it so he could better ravage Titus' mouth.

The ravaging went both ways. Titus wasn't a passive kisser. He bit and battled for dominance as he kissed. It turned Draven on something fierce.

Draven's cock was going to burst through his jeans if he got any harder. He reached around and gripped Titus' ass.

Titus moaned and turned his head aside enough to speak. "Fuck me, Draven. Please, fuck me!"

Draven wasn't an idiot. He wouldn't say no to that request. "Missed you," his traitorous mouth said, which wasn't what Draven was supposed to say. He'd meant to agree, and that confession had just...slipped out.

"Oh, god, me too. Missed you so much." Titus peppered his face with kisses. "So glad you're here."

Draven kissed him again, then he pulled, and Titus got the message. He hoisted his legs up, locking them around Draven's hips.

"Bedroom's to the left," Titus murmured before he began licking Draven's neck.

"We should talk—" Draven shut up at the look Titus gave him. "Later."

"Later," Titus agreed, then they were stumbling as they groped and kissed their way into Titus' bedroom.

Draven was surprised when Titus spun him around and pushed him down onto the bed. His dick grew harder and his breaths shorter at Titus' forcefulness. He didn't get a chance to do more than bounce once before Titus was on him, straddling Draven's thighs, shoving his shirt up to his pits, then kissing Draven with a dominance that had Draven crying out in need. He grabbed at Titus, gripping his ass as Titus began rutting against him.

Titus pinched Draven's nipples and bit his bottom lip. Draven jolted and arched, unable to be still or silent as he called out Titus' name.

Another pinch, a twist, and Titus began sucking up a mark on Draven's neck.

Draven's body seemed to be functioning in lust-mode. He wasn't capable of doing anything but letting his baser needs rule. He found the button and zip on Titus' jeans and quickly worked them open. Titus' thick cock bobbed out.

No underwear — fuck!

"Yeah," Titus murmured before nipping Draven's neck.

Draven slid his hands around to Titus' bare ass. He tracked Titus' crease with his fingertips, and Titus moaned, then he was moving again, up on his haunches, whipping his shirt off and tossing it aside, rising on one knee, pulling at his pants.

Draven helped, sitting up and nearly toppling Titus over at first, then he helped him balance and as soon as Titus was naked, Titus attacked Draven's belt and pants, his fingers a blur as he got to Draven's cock.

Draven started to mention the condoms, but Titus bolted off the bed and bent over, giving Draven a glorious view of his ass and pucker. Titus stood and had a condom and lube packet in hand.

"Prepared," Titus said, reduced to one-word sentences, which was more than Draven could manage.

Titus opened the first package then rolled the condom down Draven's cock. He jacked it a couple of times, and Draven hissed. "Close!" He *could* get a word out, when necessary, after all.

Titus opened the lube, reached behind himself then was climbing onto the bed, straddling Draven again.

Without a word said between them, their gazes locked together, and Draven *knew*. He knew this man was it for him, was the one who would take his heart and cradle it or break it.

He was utterly terrified and excited at the same time. He didn't get to examine either emotion long because Titus fisted his cock, holding it up, then began to press his hole against it.

Draven's mouth went dry as he placed his hands on Titus' thighs. Titus bore down, and the tight, hot grip of his rim, then his inner walls, drove a strangled shout from Draven.

Titus didn't go slowly. He pushed, his ass slapping Draven's groin and, just as fast, Titus rose again. He braced himself on Draven's chest, fingers scraping at Draven's nipples as Titus began riding him hard, fast, mercilessly.

Draven didn't want mercy. He cursed and bucked up, moving his hands to Titus' hips so he could help Titus slam back down.

Draven dug his heels in and fucked Titus with all the strength he had.

It wasn't enough. He growled and rolled them over, then pulled out, flipped Titus onto his belly, parted Titus' ass with one hand and used the other to guide his cock back into the tight heat of Titus' body.

Titus reared up onto his knees, shoved back and they were lost in fucking, Draven pounding into Titus, holding his hips so hard he'd probably leave bruises.

Titus began to grunt, "More," every few thrusts, and Draven gave him everything — slamming into him over and over, faster, rougher, need building, heating his skin, his insides, until Draven thought he'd combust.

He changed the angle of his hips, and Titus bellowed. Draven reached under him, fisted Titus' dick and started jacking him off.

Titus shouted, and his inner walls clenched around Draven's dick. Draven bent over him, bit Titus' nape and hot cum spurted over Draven's hand. Titus' ass went so tight around Draven's cock that there was no holding back.

Draven's head spun, and he might have screamed as he rammed his hips forward, burying his shaft as deeply in Titus as possible. Each spurt of cum felt like it boiled up from his gut, jetted to his balls then erupted from his dick.

Draven was absolutely stripped when his climax began to ebb. He'd never had such a core-shattering orgasm before, and he'd already had amazing ones with Titus.

If he'd had any hidden doubts about making a long-distance relationship with Titus work, they'd all been incinerated by that release.

Titus was his. He was Titus'. Titus might not know it yet, but Draven was going to convince him that they were it for each other.

Although, when he caught a glimpse of Titus' expression, the bliss and affection there, Draven wondered if Titus hadn't already come to the same conclusion.

Chapter Seventeen

Talking wasn't the priority it had been. Titus couldn't get enough of Draven and he knew the feeling was mutual. Titus shivered as he felt Draven's heartbeat beneath his palm. "Don't think I can move. Everything hurts perfectly."

Draven snorted and placed his hand over Titus'. "Totally fucked out."

"Yeah." Titus let his eyes drift shut. "You staying here tonight?"

"If that's okay?"

Titus had to peek up at Draven. "Is there even any question about it being okay? We're supposed to have a serious talk anyway, right?"

"I want this to work," Draven answered after a moment. "It's not just sex, either. I like *you*."

"Ditto," Titus whispered.

"So we're going to…to date? Be a couple?" Draven asked. He moved, and Titus bit back a sigh, propping himself up on one elbow and giving up on the idea of passing out just yet.

Draven was watching him, and there was so much hope in his pretty eyes that Titus felt himself tumbling over an emotional edge he wasn't ready to examine. "Yeah, be a couple. Um." Oh, and here came the hard part! "I'm not—no one here knows—"

"You're not out," Draven finished for him. "You said something along those lines. So how will this work?"

Titus bit his bottom lip. He didn't want Draven to feel like—or be—a dirty secret. There was nothing dirty about him, or what he and Titus had and did together.

But Titus *did* live in a small, conservative Texas town. He had no doubt he'd be out of a job in no time once it became public knowledge that he was gay.

"Hey." Draven cupped his cheek, and Titus realized at some point, Draven had sat up, his back against the headboard. "We don't have to figure everything out yet."

"But—" Titus couldn't stop himself from rubbing his cheek against Draven's palm.

"You said Stacy and Michelle aren't out," Draven added. "They make it work. We can, too."

But Titus didn't want to hide Draven, or his relationship with him. Although, it might be prudent to make sure they could actually *have* a relationship that would endure more than a few weeks.

Even so, Titus knew one thing. "If we make it, if…if we end up really caring for each other, I don't want to hide that, even if it means I might lose my job. I'm not ashamed of who I am, and I refuse to be ashamed of who I love." He felt himself blush. "I-if I fall in love, I mean."

Draven's smile warmed him inside, from the top of his head to the tips of his toes.

"Will people notice a guy showing up at your house often?" Draven ran his thumb over Titus' bottom lip. "Will they get suspicious?"

Titus gulped, not from fear, but because his worn-out body was trying to respond to Draven's caress. "People talk. Not much else to do in this town."

Draven's smile dimmed then flipped into a frown. "Even dating puts your job at risk."

"I'm willing to take that chance," Titus replied. "It's my choice to make."

"But you've never been out here, never dated anyone," Draven pressed.

Titus sat up all the way. "Well, no. I wasn't sure I'd ever want to date anyone again, and I told you, I'm not big on one-night stands. I guess I figured I'd just... I don't know. I honestly don't know what I was thinking." He glanced at Draven. "I had a...a bad experience with someone. I don't want to talk about it right now. It was bad enough that I thought I'd rather be celibate than let anyone near me again."

Draven growled. "Someone hurt you?"

Titus shrugged. "Don't we all get hurt at some point?" He wasn't sure that was a good question to ask. "Did—?"

Draven surprised him with a kiss, and Titus turned toward him, his question forgotten as Draven's tongue speared into him. Titus framed Draven's face with his hands and was soon straddling Draven's hips, kissing him harder, need curling hot and tight in his gut.

Titus' body wasn't as exhausted as he'd thought it was. Draven fisted both of their cocks and within minutes, both of them came, their kisses sloppy and breaths stuttering.

Somehow, Titus managed to stumble to the bathroom for another damp washcloth. Draven was asleep that fast, snoring softly as Titus wiped him clean. Titus took care of the mess on himself, then dropped the washcloth onto the floor.

He was aware that Draven had cut him off from asking if someone had hurt him, but since Titus didn't want to discuss his past, he couldn't fault Draven for feeling the same way.

But the knowledge that someone *had* gotten close enough to Draven to make him not want to talk about the pain—well, that bothered Titus like an itch he couldn't scratch.

It was hypocritical, he knew that. Draven had every right to his secrets, just like Titus did.

Still, Titus lay awake far too long, worrying over Draven's pain, and wondering if he'd moved past the man who'd caused it.

Chapter Eighteen

Draven bit back a groan when Riveen flopped down beside him. "Don't start," Draven warned.

Riveen smacked him on the arm. "Shut up. Starting is exactly what I do. So gimme the details. Did you fuck the entire forty-eight hours you were with Titus? Can he walk? Can *you*? Anyone take on a pretzel-shape?"

"Rive," Draven growled. "I'm not telling you anything about what we did!"

"But I didn't get laid. I need excitement," Riveen wheedled. "And you're my big brother, *and* you're leader of our school."

"There's four of us," Draven threw in. "I'd hardly call that a school."

"It's a school and you damn well know it," Riveen snapped. "Could you imagine if there was a large school of"—he glanced around them—"manta rays around Port A? It'd be all over the news. But just because it's small doesn't mean us four don't make a school!"

Draven prayed for a modicum of patience. "I'm not the leader. I've never been officially appointed."

"Oh my gods, *puh-leeze*. Times are changing. Things aren't done in the ocean like they were back in the old days," Riveen snarked. "It's the twenty-first century, remember? Now stop diverting and tell me how it went with Titus!"

Draven dug his toes into the sand and stared out at the waves. "Perfect," he admitted. "Rive, everything about him just...works for me. And I think I do it for him, too."

Riveen made a face. "Wait, I asked for sex details, not mushy stuff. I already know your heart goes pitter-patter because of Titus. How big is his—?"

Draven twisted and had his brother in a headlock in a matter of seconds. "Stop asking me shit like that!"

"Never," Riveen muttered, then he jabbed his fingers into Draven's side.

Draven yelped and scrambled away from Riveen and his evil fingers. "Stay back!"

"Just *tell* me," Riveen whined, waggling his fingers at Draven. "Are you in luuuuurve? Is that why you won't share the deets?"

Draven opened his mouth up to deny it, but the words wouldn't come.

Riveen laughed and clapped his hands as he did a little dance. "I knew it! He's your forever man, right?"

Draven had thought he'd had his man once before, had believed in love and truth, in destiny, and it'd almost cost him and his...school...their lives. Had almost cost Riveen his and something in Draven had shattered at the betrayal.

"Hey, Drave, don't get all moody and broody," Riveen said, nudging Draven's hip. "I can see the past washing over you like someone dumped a bucket full of seagull shit on your head."

That bit of poetry snapped Draven out of the past. "You should really just...not. Period. Don't speak. Ever again."

Riveen scrunched up his nose. "What? You don't like the bucket of seagull shit? It could happen, as much as those fuckers like to crap."

Draven shook his head. "Why, exactly, are we having this discussion?"

"Because you're in love and don't want to admit it," Riveen sang — badly. "Instead, you want to think about that lying piece of shit from your past. Let it go, bro. He's gone. Permanently." The hard glint in Riveen's eyes would have surprised most people — he only let them see his jokester side.

But Draven knew his brother well. Riveen was light-hearted most of the time — and deadly when he needed to be. However, Riveen had never been in love, or even close to it. "That's easy to say when you don't carry the scars."

"Stop being so emo. Jeez." Riveen glanced up at the sky. "I may not have ever been in love, but I have loved. You, our sibs, Mom and Dad, the aunts and uncles and so on. I know what love is, and *you* know what I'd do for love. So maybe don't worry that you love Titus. Maybe treasure that, and thank the gods you got another chance, with a good man. One who will probably freak out over your secret, but not try to sell you out. It's been almost fifty years."

And now there were so many new ways shifters were endangered.

Draven studied his brother's profile. Riveen was indisputably attractive, yet he'd never had a relationship that lasted longer than a few fucks. "Why haven't you found someone?"

"Because I haven't looked." Riveen shrugged before turning to him. "This is my last pep talk for you, Drave, so don't fuck this up with Titus. He's a good guy. I like him. You know I hated shit-for-brains." Riveen's flinch was miniscule, but Draven saw it.

Riveen *had* hated Andres — that didn't mean he had no regrets about killing him.

Draven slipped one arm around his brother's shoulders. He didn't say thank you — he'd done that years ago, and Riveen wouldn't appreciate it being said again. "I won't give you details, but I *will* admit that we didn't get out of bed except to shower or eat."

Riveen snorted. "Wow, boring. You could have at least had more variety and fucked in other places! I don't want your details after all."

"Someone hurt him," Draven said as they began strolling along the beach. "I didn't pry. Wouldn't have wanted him poking around in my past, but…"

"Buuuut, it's making you crazy not knowing what happened," Riveen surmised. "Understandable. Although, don't you think most people have been hurt by his age? He's handsome, and he was single for a while. It was because he's chosen to be alone, not because he couldn't find someone to date or whatever. What would be the reason for that except he'd had his heart broken before?"

"I hate this unknown guy who hurt him," Draven muttered. "Fucker."

Riveen cackled. "I bet Titus would hate your ex, too. Isn't that kind of like a relationship rule? Got to hate the exes unless they've remained friends. Then it's just awkward. Or I think it'd be awkward. I don't want to find a man then have to be buds with whoever he's had sex with. I'd be too jealous."

"Maybe if you loved him that you'd just be happy, period," Draven suggested.

Riveen rolled his eyes so hard, Draven was surprised there wasn't some kind of noise coming from his eye sockets.

"I am perfectly happy now, single and happy," Riveen declared. "Well, I'd be happier if I got laid. Or had some ice cream."

"I can help you with one of those things."

Riveen snickered. "Ohhh, you perv!"

Draven couldn't help but laugh. "Gross. So gross. I meant we can get ice cream."

Riveen sighed and covered his heart with one hand. "Thank Triton. I was afraid even you weren't immune to my charms, and those days of siblings marrying to keep on ruling are long gone."

"That also never applied to our kind," Draven pointed out. "And I'm not the only one immune to your charms. Titus didn't fall for you."

"That's 'cause Titus is smart and chose well," Riveen said.

Before Draven could ask why Riveen had just insulted himself, Riveen took off at a run.

"Last one there buys!"

Draven glared as he bolted into a run. "Cheater!"

Riveen's laughter made him smile, and Draven wasn't even mad when he ended up having to buy Riveen a triple scoop waffle cone.

"So when are you going to see him again?" Riveen asked after he'd licked his ice cream.

"He's coming here tomorrow," Draven said. "Three days apart. It shouldn't seem so hard to be without him for that short a period of time."

Riveen just grinned at him, and Draven wasn't embarrassed by his admission. There was no reason to be. Riveen was happy for him, and some day, Draven would be the one grinning and teasing Riveen about falling in love.

Chapter Nineteen

Titus took a sip of his water while he stared out at the hummingbirds flitting around in Stacy and Michelle's back yard.

"You can't live in Texas and not drink sweet tea," Michelle teased. "Seriously, they'll throw you out of the state."

Titus shrugged. "Hey, if that's the way it has to be, then…" He hated Texas tea.

Michelle shook her head. "You poor, misguided man. You don't know what you're missing."

Titus chuckled but he wasn't missing a what—he was missing Draven. *We haven't known each other long. Don't really know each other. I can't be this…attached.*

Who was he kidding? He'd been hooked on Draven probably from the first night they'd been together. He'd just tried to suppress that truth from himself because he'd thought Draven would want to stick with keeping to the vacation-fling plan.

But he hadn't, and Titus was so damned glad that Draven had showed up in town. He'd come to Titus, like some romantic lead in a movie. Titus' heart was all but in Draven's hands. If he wasn't fully in love with him yet —

"You keep getting this far-off look," Stacy said, drawing Titus out of his thoughts. "Are you thinking about your summer stud?"

For one second, Titus thought Stacy had caught on to Draven having shown up. But she didn't know and was referring to their time together at the coast. Titus didn't want to go there, not explicitly, but he stalled as he was considering what to share with his friends. "I was watching the smaller hummingbird dive-bomb that bigger one. Those little suckers are vicious."

"They are," Stacy agreed, "and you keep on not telling us about your fling, and we'll keep getting more suspicious by the day that it wasn't just a fling after all."

Titus traced a pattern on his glass, watching his fingertip rather than looking at his friends. "I don't want to fuck and tell, but yeah. I really like Draven."

"Like, not liked?" Stacy prodded. She leaned close to him. "So, is there something you want to share?"

Titus finally glanced at her. "Yes. Like. We've decided to try and give dating a chance."

Stacy squealed and twisted around to high-five Michelle. "Told you! I *told* you there was going to be more to them than just a fling! No one in their right mind could let Titus go."

Titus hoped he didn't flinch. Luckily, Stacy and Michelle weren't looking at him until he forced himself to continue as if he hadn't been interrupted. "And we don't really live that far apart. I think maybe he and I could —" His phone blared with a tone that startled him then made him freeze, fear coalescing in his gut. Then he went numb when his brain processed why fear had kicked in.

"Titus?" Stacy was beside him, cupping his face in her hands. "Titus, what's wrong? Who's calling? Let me see your phone. I'll rip them a new one!"

"Not a call," he forced out as he tried to remain calm. "Message. Message tone. Alert. Only one setting for it." He trembled as he retrieved his phone from the pocket of his shorts. All he had to do was look at it, and nausea hit him. Titus dropped the phone, shot up out of the chair and ran for the bathroom.

"VINE? What's VINE? Shit!" he heard Stacy exclaim. "Titus!"

Titus made it to the bathroom and slid to his knees in front of the toilet. The dinner he'd had came up instantly, and his eyes and nose burned. Stacy would figure out what VINE was—the victim notification program that let victims know when their offender was being released from prison.

Titus heaved again and broke out in goosebumps. His mind reeled back to that night almost five years ago. "No," he whispered. He'd known at some point this day would come, had thought he'd be prepared for it.

He'd been wrong.

Chapter Twenty

Draven was thrilled that Titus was arriving a day early. They'd been apart a week. It'd felt like longer. When he'd gotten Titus' text asking if it was okay to show up today, Draven had almost shouted with joy. And, *of course,* Riveen had been with him, and given him a smug look that had made Draven want to trip his smart-ass brother.

Luckily, Riveen had been distracted by a "Shiny" — Draven didn't even want to guess what Riveen was referring to in such a way—and had left in a bit of a rush.

Well, maybe Draven would have something to tease Riveen about in the near future.

Draven kept peeking out through the front window to see if Titus had arrived. God, he was pathetic, and so hooked on Titus, it wasn't funny. Draven's heart raced every time he thought of the man, and Titus was always on his mind.

Which should have scared Draven more than it did. He'd been hurt before, but… *But Titus isn't like him. And this doesn't feel the same.*

Before he could fret anymore, he saw Titus' blue car turning into the driveway. Draven's smile probably looked goofy, but he didn't care as he opened the front door then loped down the steps. He couldn't wait to get his arms around Titus!

Titus parked the car and unbuckled. Draven's smile faltered as he caught a glimpse of something in Titus' expression. It wasn't happiness, that was certain. Draven opened Titus' door, and Titus gave him a weary look.

"What's wrong?" Draven had a split-second of panic that Titus had changed his mind about them dating, but he quickly dispelled the notion. Titus wouldn't have wanted to get there early just to dump Draven. *Which means something else is wrong.*

Draven held out a hand to Titus. "Tell me."

Titus blinked. "My bag…"

"I'll get it while you talk to me."

Titus got out of the car. "Could you kiss me first?"

Draven's jangling nerves settled a little at that. He guessed he'd still been worried that he was about to get dumped, despite his reasoning. For an answer, Draven pulled Titus into his arms, then slanted his mouth over Titus'.

It was amazing how perfectly Titus fit against him, how warm and strong he was, how incredible he tasted. Everything about him was perfect for Draven, even his flaws. Draven hadn't found any of those yet, but he knew, like every living person, Titus had to have some.

And they wouldn't matter to Draven. He slid one hand down to massage the small of Titus' back as he deepened the kissed.

Titus clung to him, there was no other way to describe it. Draven could almost taste his desperation, and Titus trembled as he caressed him.

Draven eased his head back just enough to break the kiss. He opened his eyes and saw that Titus still had his closed. Titus' lips were parted, and his cheeks flushed. A soft whimper slipped from him, and Draven kissed him again, letting go of his thoughts and immersing himself in everything Titus.

He couldn't get enough of this one man, didn't think such a thing was possible. Draven slid one hand down and cupped Titus' ass, giving it a good squeeze.

Titus pressed closer to him.

A horn blared, and Titus jolted. He probably would have stumbled back had Draven let go of him.

"Just someone honking," Draven rasped. "Not at us. Down the road, sounded like."

Titus gulped and nodded. "I…" He pressed his lips together and all that electric need that had been flowing between them was shut off. "We need to talk."

Draven slowly let go of Titus until only one hand lingered on Titus' shoulder. "What's wrong?"

Titus shuddered. "Can we go inside?"

"Of course." Draven didn't want to stop touching Titus. Whatever was bothering him had to be pretty bad. Now Draven could see it all over Titus — 'it' being his nervousness and something that sure looked like fear. "I'll get your bag and we can go in. Trunk?" Just as he asked it, he saw the duffel in the back seat. "Oh. I see it."

Draven moved his hand to Titus' waist, then put his arm around his lover's hips. He needed Titus close, and he thought that was what Titus needed, too, judging by how Titus moved closer to him.

After Draven had grabbed the bag, Titus locked the car. Draven nudged him to take the steps first, since walking up them side by side wasn't possible. Titus reached behind him, and Draven slipped his hand into Titus'. Worry quickly filled Draven. Something was definitely wrong, and it wasn't a problem with Draven. *Maybe someone in his town found out about us?*

Titus went inside, and Draven was right behind him. Draven didn't stop any longer than it took for Titus to lock the front door—something Draven didn't think Titus had done there before—then Draven was leading Titus into the master bedroom. "Tell me what's wrong," Draven urged as he tossed the duffel bag onto the chair by the window.

Titus shuddered again, and Draven sat on the bed. "Come here and I'll hold you while you tell me."

"That'd be—" Titus licked his lips, more of a nervous action than a sensual one. "That'd be good."

Draven kicked off his flip flops, moved the pillows up against the headboard then got comfortable. Titus removed his shoes and crawled up onto the bed. He surprised Draven by lying on his belly almost, with one leg thrown over Draven's and resting his right arm over Draven's stomach. Titus used Draven's chest for a pillow.

"What's wrong?" Draven asked, sliding his fingers through Titus' soft hair. "Did someone find out?"

Titus took a deep breath then let it out. "That's not— I mean, I told Stacy and Michelle, but they're cool. Remember how I mentioned I hadn't been with anyone in a long time? Years. I moved somewhere I wouldn't even be tempted to get involved. Small, conservative town."

Draven's gut pitched and went cold. "Why'd you do that?" Titus had said as much before, but Draven hadn't focused on it. He'd just thought Titus — well, he hadn't thought about it, had he? "Baby, please?"

Titus tipped his head back and kissed Draven's neck. "I'm scared. Not of you," he added, his breath ghosting over Draven's skin. "Never of you."

Draven kept his touch gentle as he sought to comfort Titus. "I'll never hurt you." And he knew then why Titus was trying not to fall apart. "Who did? Who hurt you?"

Titus clenched his fist, grasping a handful of Draven's shirt. "You hear about domestic abuse all the time. It's hard to admit, to accept, that it happened to me. My boyfriend — first one, only one until…"

Draven finished for him when Titus seemed unable or perhaps afraid to. "Until me."

"Yeah." Titus kissed him again. "I mean, I'd messed around some before I met Joel when I was a freshman at UTSA. He was…overwhelming, maybe. I don't know. Older, a senior, handsome. I didn't know why he was interested in me. Why he was single."

Draven already wanted to beat Joel into a bloody puddle.

Titus' laugh held more bitterness than not. "Now I know why. He needed a certain type of guy. Someone who was easy to manipulate. I was so shy, and no one talked to me. I was the perfect victim for someone like him."

Draven tried to remain calm, to keep himself from tensing up as anger pulsed through him.

"We started dating after he asked me out several times. I thought he was just screwing with me. He was…dynamic. Handsome. Wealthy. I didn't know what he saw in me," Titus said again. "He had to work to get me to agree to a coffee date in the cafeteria. He seemed so nice, so focused on me. By the time I moved in with him in my sophomore year, I thought I was in love with him. I guess I was, just…just the version of him he showed me. I should have known it was all wrong. Everything was perfect…well, that's how I felt. The little corrections Joel suggested for me were only meant to help me not be so awkward and shy."

"Titus," Draven whispered, aching for the young man he could easily imagine Titus to be back then. Innocent, trusting, wanting the love and affection he thought was being offered, when in truth, he'd been manipulated by—

"It didn't start out as physical violence until I'd lived with Joel for almost a year. He would snap at me then tell me it was for my own good. I was too soft, too easily hurt," Titus murmured. "I needed thicker skin. I believed him. I knew I was socially off. Then he came home one night, and when I didn't get up to meet him at the door because I was working on a term paper, he grabbed me by the hair and punched me in the stomach."

As Titus began to tremble again, Draven held him closer and dropped kisses into his hair. "I'm so sorry, baby." He wasn't sure what else to say. If he bellowed with the rage he felt, that'd be no help to Titus.

"He usually kept the bruises to places I could easily cover," Titus said after a moment. "But he got more violent, and I wanted to leave. I tried once, and he found me at the hotel on the south side of San Antonio.

I still don't know how. After he got me back to his place, after what he did, I didn't try to leave again. I'd probably be dead if he hadn't lost it when we were dining at his favorite restaurant. It was my senior year then, and I don't even know what set him off. I saw it click, though, that furious glint in his eyes that always appeared before he hit me. I knew when we got home, I was going to pay for whatever made him mad. Maybe I picked up the wrong fork, I really don't know. He jerked me out of my chair and slapped me. I was so stunned. He'd never hit my face before then. I remember people gasping, then—just pain. He hit me, and someone tried to stop him. A woman. My lawyer said that's probably why Joel got as many years as he did, because he hit her, broke her nose and cheek bone. And all he was sentenced to was eight years, five served. I guess he got out early because he behaved or whatever. I got the text yesterday that he was being released and I can't—I feel like I'm going to shake out of my skin."

"I'm here," Draven murmured. "I won't let anyone hurt you, Titus. I swear it." If he had to move to the small town where Titus lived, then so be it.

"I shouldn't be scared. I should be able to defend myself against him."

Titus' quiet sob tore at Draven's heart as he struggled to find the right words. None came. He wanted to find Joel whatever-his-name-was and break him in two.

"Stay with me for the summer?" Draven asked instead, the question just blurted out before he'd even coherently formed the thought of it. "We can go back to your place if you have to do anything for work. Just, stay with me and..." *And what? Relax?* Draven bit back a groan at his own ineptitude. "Please. I'd like you to. I missed you this week. I'm not just asking because of what you told me." *Total truth. Gods, I want him here, or I want to be with him wherever. I just need him.* But he didn't want to cling too tight and remind Titus of Joel. "You don't have to. We can keep dating and—"

"If you mean it," Titus said so quietly that Draven almost didn't hear him. "Maybe for a little while, at least."

"Yes." Draven would take "*a little while*" and hope it turned into forever. He nuzzled Titus' hair and asked him if he wanted to talk about anything else that happened with Joel. It made Draven's gut burn to do so, but Titus' hesitant, "Yes," told Draven he'd done the right thing, and no matter how hard it would be, he'd listen to every detail of what Titus needed to share with him.

Chapter Twenty-One

Titus liked the way Draven held his hand as they walked along the beach. "I'm glad we got up to see the sunrise."

Draven nodded. "It's something few people appreciate. I know sleeping in is great, but this" — he gestured toward the sky, which was growing brighter with a myriad of colors — "this touches the soul." Then he blushed darkly and turned his head aside.

Titus touched Draven's hot cheek. "Don't be embarrassed. That was beautiful, and fitting. I like you being, well, *you*."

Draven looked at him and smiled, a shy quirk of his lips that did funny things to Titus' belly.

"Just don't tell my brother, okay?" Draven said. "He'd never let me live it down that I have a...um...poetic side, maybe."

"I promise not to narc," Titus assured him as a wave trickled over his toes. "Water's so warm."

"Want to go for a swim?"

Titus chuckled. Draven was *always* up for a swim. "Sure. Last one in's a rotten egg!" He tugged his hand free and ran into the ocean—which worked about as well as running through wet cement after a few steps.

He didn't even have time to do more than shriek when Draven caught him with an arm around his waist. Draven whooped and turned, then they were both going down, salt water and sand all around them.

They hadn't gotten deep enough for them to be in any danger. Titus rolled to his knees, Draven beside him, as they both laughed and swiped at their faces, pushing aside hair and water. "You turd!"

Draven snorted. "That's a teacher insult for sure. No bad words allowed."

"Even 'turd' is bad if I say it around kids or parents," Titus replied. "My grandma always said, never say something you wouldn't want a mouth full of."

"That..." Draven frowned. "That doesn't make sense, actually. I don't want a mouth full of sand, or money, or—"

Titus chuckled and poked Draven. "Um, you would *not* have argued with my grandma. She'd have skinned you alive. Possibly literally."

Draven looked skeptical. "Really? I don't think she would have *literally* done that."

"Hah. You have no idea. Grandma was not someone to be messed with," Titus said. "Now, my other grandma is as sweet as Texas tea. She can't swat a fly, and yes, I mean *that* literally, too. Poor Grandpa has to take care of the flies when she isn't around."

"Hm. And your other grandpa? The one who was, er, with the skinning grandma?"

"That was Grandma Eleanor. She divorced my grandpa way back before I was born. Dad never really knew him." Titus shrugged. "He died in Vietnam. I think maybe Grandma Eleanor regretted divorcing him, but I don't know. And she wasn't mean, just firm. She passed away a few years back. Grandma Janet and Grandpa Ed are both still alive and healthy. They live outside of Austin where a bunch of my cousins are. Well, and a couple of aunts, hence the cousins. Anyway, what about you? I don't think you've ever really talked about anyone in your family other than Riveen."

Draven snorted. "Isn't he enough?"

Titus wondered if Draven were trying to divert from the question, but before he could consider it, something brushed against his calf. "Eek!" And he sounded like a dork as he scrambled away from whatever it was that had touched him.

"Damn it," Draven muttered, tugging Titus close.

"What?" Titus twisted around, his panic vanishing as common sense told him he'd probably just had a seaweed encounter.

Except it wasn't seaweed behind him. "Oh my god!" Titus moved faster than he ever had in his life, grabbing hold of Draven's arm and shooting to his feet.

"Titus, it's not going to hurt you," Draven rumbled, though he stood as well and took a few steps before he dug in his heels. "It's just a manta ray."

Titus gulped and had to either stop trying to run with Draven, or let Draven go. He stopped and turned enough to glare at Draven. "*Just* a manta ray?"

The creature was right behind Draven! "Draven!"

Draven kicked the water, splashing it at the manta ray. "Cut it out. Go do manta ray things."

The manta ray splashed Draven back, then thumped his leg before spinning around in a circle.

"Why isn't it going away?" Titus hated how shaky his voice sounded. "It's huge and it needs to *go away!*" He'd seen articles and clips of people swimming with manta rays but had assumed those were somehow…tamed. This one was entirely too close to Draven. "Shoo!"

Titus could have sworn the thing looked at him and laughed. Air bubbles floated up to the surface of the water.

"Get," Draven snapped, and the manta ray finally made a lazy spin off toward the deeper water and left them alone.

"I didn't know those were in the water," Titus mumbled, eyes glued to the last spot he'd seen the creature at. "Not here. I thought they were in the Pacific, or Atlantic, or just…just deeper water. We've been swimming with those?"

"Sometimes there's a few of them around the Gulf Coast area," Draven said, and he seemed to be studying Titus closely. "They don't hurt anyone. Mantas are peaceful, and they usually avoid humans."

"That one didn't." Titus shivered despite the warmth of the water and the day. "They don't have the spiny tails, right?"

"No, they don't have the defensive barbs like a stingray does," Draven agreed. "They can bite, but honestly, they stay away from people if they can, so biting isn't an issue. That one, I've fed before. Regrettably."

Titus cocked his head and kept staring at the water. "So it's friendly?"

Draven snorted. "It's a damned pest, but yeah."

"Not sure I want to swim with it," Titus mused. "You might be all chill about it, but I'm nervous, to put it mildly."

Draven muttered something under his breath, then he slipped his hand into Titus' grasp. "It won't bother you again."

Titus wasn't sure how Draven could make that promise, but...he was inclined to believe him.

Chapter Twenty-Two

After all that Titus had confided in him, Draven wanted to share his past but for the life of him, couldn't figure out how. Him being a shifter was a big part of it, along with the betrayal and threat to him and his kind, his loved ones. Andres had broken Draven's belief in love, but Titus was swiftly building it back up.

Draven rubbed at his chest as he studied Titus' profile. Titus was talking on the phone with Stacy. He was tense, with his shoulders tight and a pinched expression in place. Even so, he was handsome, and Draven's breath hitched when Titus suddenly relaxed and smiled.

Must mean his house and everything's okay. Draven knew Titus was worried Joel would show up, though he had said Joel hadn't contacted him from prison. Draven wasn't sure if that just meant Joel had had more time to stew in his sadistic hatefulness or if he'd moved on with plans to find someone else to beat.

In Draven's experiences — albeit they were limited to observances of other people's lives — abusers didn't change. He'd heard some claims here and there that one got help and was a changed person, but he would never believe it. Anyone who could hurt another being and make them feel like they had no value was not redeemable.

The world wasn't so black and white. Draven needed to work on the in-between shades that were more numerous than the starker ends of the spectrum. Regardless, he had a problem with abusive assholes — especially now that he knew Titus had been victimized by one and was still living in fear of him.

Draven fisted his hands even as he worked to keep his expression calm. He had some friends — well, Riveen did, mainly. Draven wasn't as chatty. He *did* have some shifter family and friends he could reach out to for help, though. Riven, always the life of the party, had many more. Between the both of them, they might be able to find out where Joel was.

Of course, it'd help if Draven had a last name for the fucker.

And he wasn't going to tell anyone else Titus' personal business unless Titus said it was okay.

Draven bit his bottom lip as he thought about that. He needed to find a way to tell Titus who he was, what he was, rather, and about his own past. The idea made Draven's gut burn like he'd swallowed acid — and not the fun kind, either.

Titus had been spooked by Riveen — *asshole* — earlier in the morning.

But he hadn't kept running. After Draven had started talking to him, Titus hadn't kept trying to drag him out of the sea. Yes, Titus might be leery of getting in the water now, but that didn't mean he *wouldn't* get in. Draven understood how much of a shock it must have been to see Riveen pop up like that.

And Draven knew what Riveen was up to. He was trying to get Draven to tell Titus he was a shifter.

Draven tried playing that scenario out in his head then stopped himself short. Titus had enough stress in his life right now. Adding to that might not be the best thing to do. And what were his true intentions in telling Titus? To remove the chunk of guilt over hiding the secret? Because hurting Titus or scaring him to make himself feel better was unacceptable.

So Draven decided he'd think it over some more, and see how Titus felt before dropping the bombshell that shifters existed and Draven was one of them.

He'd do what was best for Titus because he needed to put Titus first.

Titus chuckled and flapped one hand. He was an animated person on the phone and was adorable to watch. Draven was gawking like a starved man staring at a steak, but he couldn't bring himself to stop it.

Then Titus turned, and their eyes met. Draven flushed with warmth and some happy, bright sensation that he knew meant he was heart over heinie for Titus.

"Gotta go," Titus murmured, gaze locked with Draven's. "Yeah. Later." He disconnected the call, tossed the phone onto the counter then sauntered over to Draven.

Words weren't necessary. Draven reached for him, cupping Titus' nape and hip, pulling him close and kissing him. There was no holding back. Draven showed Titus all his want, all of his need. Draven was trembling, shivers racing down his spine as the importance of the man in his arms truly sunk into him.

He loved Titus, without a doubt, and with the deep, soul-penetrating love that people usually only dreamed of having. Something in him recognized something in Titus. Draven couldn't pinpoint it or name it, but he knew it was true.

Draven tugged at the back of Titus' shirt. He wanted all the clothing gone—Titus', his. He needed skin. It meant breaking apart for a few precious seconds, but Draven pulled back and whipped off Titus' shirt. Then he had his own off, along with his shorts. Titus was nude just as quickly, and Draven reached for him, moaning when he finally got the contact he craved.

Titus clutched at his biceps as Draven kissed him without finesse or restraint. They moved, stumbling because they wouldn't let go of each other, wouldn't stop kissing on the way over to the couch.

Draven wanted to take his time, but he also needed to be inside Titus *now*.

Titus raked his blunt nails up and over Draven's shoulders, not hurting him, but bringing a delicious sting and sensitizing Draven's skin.

This was going to be fast and dirty.

Draven didn't have a condom at hand, but that was okay. He broke the kiss and spun Titus around, then bent him over the back of the couch. As soon as he had Titus in place, Draven pressed one finger between Titus' cheeks and rubbed over his hole.

Titus hissed and arched his lower back. He spread his knees, giving Draven an erotic view that stole his breath. He bent and licked his way down Titus' crease to his tight little pucker.

"Oh...god—" Titus broke off with a whimper when Draven licked him.

Draven pressed Titus' cheeks apart, then rimmed Titus until Titus' hole loosened and Titus was begging him for more.

"Suck," Draven ordered, offering Titus two fingers.

Titus moaned as he sealed his lips around them.

Draven's cock ached. He was dangerously close to coming just from what he was doing to Titus.

Titus flicked his tongue between Draven's fingers, and Draven had to grip the base of his own shaft to suppress his release. He nipped Titus' ass as he slid his fingers free.

When he pushed them into Titus' hole, the gripping heat and silky walls contracting around his digits almost drove Draven out of his mind. He wanted to fuck Titus raw, to thrust into him and fill him with his cum.

But Draven had enough sense to hold back. He thrust his fingers deeper, harder, and Titus moaned and begged for more.

Draven curved his fingers, feeling around for Titus' gland. "Jack yourself," he managed to get out as he found it.

"Fuck!" Titus shouted. He reached for his dick and started stroking it.

Draven felt the pleasure Titus was experiencing, felt it in the way Titus' ass clenched around his fingers, the way he shoved back harder, demanding a rougher fuck.

Draven gave him what he could, pressing in hard and fast, turning his wrist, stretching Titus without pushing him too far. The next time Draven brushed over his gland, Titus keened, and a pink blush spread down from his neck to his back. His hips stuttered, and

Draven smelled his spunk as Titus came, Draven's fingers held still by Titus' gripping walls.

Draven kissed Titus' ass, his lower back, his hip, loving on Titus until Titus' climax ebbed and the clenching muscles holding Draven's fingers loosened.

Then Draven eased his digits free and spat in his hand. He spread that and the pre-cum leaking from his slit over his length before he pressed his cock between Titus' cheeks.

Titus reached back and grabbed at him as Draven fucked Titus' crease, grunting like some wild beast, unable to form a single word with the pleasure building inside him. Less than a dozen thrusts, and Draven shuddered, gasping as he came, his orgasm tearing up from deep inside him.

He couldn't keep his eyes open after the first jet splattered on Titus' back. That was too bad. He'd like to have watched. Instead, he just *felt*, shaken to his core with the intensity of his climax.

Draven was weak-kneed afterward, and he hooked one arm around Titus' hips as he collapsed on the couch.

Titus flopped down on his belly with his head in Draven's lap. "Jesus," Titus mumbled. "'Bout killed me."

Draven trailed his fingers through his cum on Titus' back. "Ditto. Can't even stand up."

Titus rumbled something and wedged one of his arms behind Draven and draped the other around his front.

Draven wanted this every day for the rest of his life. He thought Titus did, too. Their future couldn't be built on lies or secrets, however. Draven needed to tell Titus soon that he was a shifter.

He'd talk to Riveen, and a few other people, see if they could find Joel-whatever-his-name was. But even if they didn't find him soon, Draven was going to bare his soul to Titus. It wasn't for his own sake, either, because Draven knew after what they'd just shared, that Titus was as deep into the relationship as he was.

Draven wasn't falling alone, and he wouldn't hide who he was from Titus much longer.

Chapter Twenty-Three

It didn't surprise Titus that Riveen walked into the house without bothering to knock. Titus was just glad that he and Draven had showered and gotten dressed minutes earlier, because he was certain that them being naked wouldn't have stopped Riveen or embarrassed him.

"Aw, you two are so cute!" Riveen said in a syrup-sweet voice. "All cuddly and smelling like sex."

"We showered," Titus informed him, trying not to blush — to no avail.

"Rive," Draven growled, striding toward his brother. "I swear to the gods, I'll toss you down the stairs if you don't behave."

Riveen didn't appear to be the least bit intimidated as he rolled his eyes. "Yeah, right. Let me just point out that knowing you had sex, and I didn't, is punishment enough for my smart mouth."

Titus shook his head. "There are so many things wrong with your statement that I don't even know where to begin. Maybe with, that's not an apology."

"Duh." Riveen squealed and ducked when Draven swiped at him and all but pranced around to the other side of the room. "Missed me, missed me, now you gotta— Well, wrong state for that next part. We're backward in Texas, but not *that* backward. Some of the time."

"Hey, don't mess with Texas. It has some governmental issues, but the people are generally great," Titus said.

Riveen gave another eye-roll. "Calm your tits, Titus. Heh. I like that. You know if you take the U out of your name, you get tits?"

Draven growled again and started for Riveen. Titus figured the brothers needed to blow off some steam or do whatever it was brothers did. *Pick on each other, apparently.* "I'm going to get the enchiladas going." He needed food after all the calories he'd burned off coming his brains out. "You two—don't break anything."

"Just gonna break *him*," Draven called out.

Riveen cackled, and Titus left them to it. He had everything ready to make what he called 'cheater's enchiladas'. It was probably a casserole, because he was too lazy to soften the tortillas, then stuff and roll them. Instead, he used a baking dish and layered his favorite brand of beanless chili, then tortillas, a can of diced tomatoes and green chilies and lots of cheese. He kept repeating that pattern until the dish was filled, which didn't take long.

Titus crossed over to the other cabinets and took the tin foil out of the drawer—and realized there were no more sounds of horsing around coming from the living room. Instead, he caught the low murmur of voices, and he wondered what the brothers were discussing that they didn't want him to overhear.

Oh. Titus stopped mid-step and almost face-planted. *They're talking about me. Is...is Draven telling him – ?* Titus gulped and felt shame wash over him. Of *course* Draven would tell Riveen about Joel. Draven and Riven were close despite all the sniping and teasing. Or maybe because of it, Titus didn't know which.

Titus forced himself to move, to finish walking back to the dish he'd been readying for the oven. *It would have been nice if Draven had asked me if I was okay with him telling Riveen beforehand. Is this a betrayal of trust? Did I ask him not to tell anyone? Should I have had to? Where's the line between familial loyalty and – ?*

"Dude, you're gonna kill the tinfoil."

Titus startled at Riveen's voice. "What?" He blinked and saw that he'd crushed the foil he'd pulled out. Titus didn't even remember unrolling it. "Oh. Uh."

Draven was at his side in an instant. "Hey, what's wrong?" he whispered, his breath warm against Titus' ear.

Titus glanced at him then started unballing the foil. "Nothing."

"Titus." Draven touched his lower back. "Tell me."

Titus pressed his lips together.

Draven looked at his brother. "Rive, give us some privacy."

"No fucking," Riveen said before he muttered something Titus couldn't quite make out.

"Tell me what's wrong," Draven demanded, then added, "please."

Titus still didn't know if he had a right to be mad or not. "I heard you two talking a minute or two ago."

Draven stiffened beside him. "Fuck."

Titus forced himself to spread the foil over the top of the pan then place the enchiladas in the oven. All the while, Draven stood rigid like he'd been turned to stone.

Maybe I'm making too much of it. Would I have said he could tell Riveen? Well, I think I'd have have agreed after I had time to consider it. What am I upset over? That he didn't ask me first, even though I would have said yes?

When he thought about it like that, Titus felt like a jerk. He sighed and turned to lean against the counter so that he was facing Draven. Titus didn't want anger or whatever this uncomfortable feeling was that was happening between them.

"Hey." He nudged Draven's foot with his toes. "It's okay. I'm not mad."

Draven shook his head and finally looked at him. "Not mad?" He blinked. "You're not freaked out, either?"

Titus went for full-course honesty. "Well, I was at first. I don't want you to have to keep secrets from your brother, though. I do wish you'd have asked me before you told him about Joel."

Draven frowned. "What? Before I – ?" His eyes went wide. "Oh, no! No, I didn't – I wouldn't, not without discussing it with you. I thought you heard us?"

Then it was Titus' turn to frown. "What were you talking about? I thought..." He felt like an idiot. "Crap. I couldn't actually hear what was being said, just murmurs, like I wasn't supposed to be *able* to hear. I assumed, like an idiot, you were telling Riveen about...about Joel."

Draven shook his head. "But I wasn't. We were talking about family stuff." He rubbed his face with his hands. "Shit. Shit!"

Titus got a bad feeling in the pit of his belly. "Draven, it's okay. I don't have to know everything you and Riveen talk about. I made an incorrect assumption, and I'm sorry. I didn't mean to make you feel bad or to intrude."

"The thing is…" Draven took a deep breath. "The thing is — "

"Is it safe to come into the kitchen now?" Riveen bounded into the room. Draven grumbled, and Titus patted his arm.

"It's safe," Titus said. "Everything's okay."

Riveen smiled, but it wasn't quite his usual one. "Oh? So…nothing's…shifted between you two?"

"What does that mean, even?" Titus asked as Draven snarled, "Rive!"

Riveen held up his hands as if asking them to stop, though Titus didn't know what they were supposed to stop doing. "Okay, okay, I just worry about you two lovebirds. You are my inspiration, so you aren't allowed to do…whatever that was you did. No weirdness. Only love."

Only love. Titus' gaze tangled with Draven's, and yes, he knew he loved the man despite the short time they'd known each other.

He wanted to say the words, but not with Riveen right there. Titus slipped his hand in one of Draven's instead. *Later, once Riveen is gone.* He'd tell Draven that he'd fallen in love with him.

Chapter Twenty-Four

Draven was nervous. It was stupid, really, to be on edge, but he knew he was going to say those three special words to Titus tonight.

He was kind of thinking Titus had the same plan in mind. Titus kept shooting him quick glances that spoke of the same nervousness Draven was experiencing. Then there were the lingering looks, the casual, frequent touches they both shared.

And the connection between him and Titus was almost a physical thing, like a wire growing tauter by the minute, although unlike a stretched wire, the connection wasn't thinning. Rather, it was growing stronger. Draven felt it in his core, his soul, in the ancient part of what he was that knew its mate.

He'd thought Andres was the man he'd spend his life with, but what he'd had with Andres could not compare to the feelings he had for Titus. Draven didn't question why he'd been fooled before. He'd been terribly lonely and had wanted someone to commit to.

Then he'd wanted nothing more than to protect his bruised heart after Andres' betrayal.

"You need to tell him," Riveen muttered, nudging Draven's hip when Titus headed for the bathroom and left them alone. "You're already hooked. You *have* to tell him. He's not Andres. I have love cooties from the two of you eye-fucking each other all night."

"Love cooties?" Draven glared at Riveen. "You're stuck at about twelve years old, emotionally — max."

"Duh. And now I'll have to go home and scrub the cooties off before I fall for some guy with a pretty smile and a nice ass," Riveen drawled. "Like your guy."

Draven glared harder. "Stop ogling him, and shouldn't you be going home soon?"

"It'd be rude to leave while Titus is in the bathroom." Riveen stood, though, and stretched, his back popping as he arched it. "Mmm. I could use a massage. Bet I can find someone to give me one, along with giving me the big D."

Groaning, Draven rubbed at his forehead. "Jeez, Riveen. Really?"

"Was the big D too much?"

"I vote yes," Titus said, coming back into the living room. "Besides, you might end up with an average D, and there's nothing wrong with that."

Riveen gasped. "Uh, there *is*. I'm totally a size guy. Well, average length is okay. Even a little smaller, but give me a fat dick, one that makes me — "

"Riveen!" Draven snapped, coming to his feet. "Cut it out."

"Prudes, the both of you," Riveen groused. "I'm going out to get that massage. You know, an internal one along with a backrub."

Titus' groan was laced with enough amusement that Draven decided not to snarl at Riveen.

"See you later. Don't do anything crazy," Riveen said as he walked to the door. "You should be all prudish and spend the night talking. Talking's a good thing."

Draven was going to kick Riveen's ass.

Riveen rolled his eyes, as if he knew what Draven was thinking. Then Riveen cackled and left.

"Finally," Draven muttered. He sighed and sat, more nervous than he'd been minutes earlier. "Um."

Titus came over and sat beside him. "Was he trying to force you to tell me something?"

Draven gulped and found himself reaching for Titus' hands.

Titus slid his palms over Draven's easily, then twined his fingers with Draven's. "You can tell me anything. Or maybe I should tell you something."

Draven's heart pounded and he stared into Titus' pretty eyes. "I love you." The words slipped free, sweet and steady, from his mouth. All the panic and nerves settled, as if they exited his body with the admission.

Titus smiled bigger than Draven had ever seen him do, and he leaned in, brushing his lips over Draven's. "Oh, honey, I love you too. So quick, but I know it's true. I know it's good. Right. Strong."

Draven nodded, then kissed Titus deeper, freeing one hand so he could cup Titus' jaw. Heat rushed through him, desire and tenderness twining together in a perfect blend.

Draven reveled in the taste of Titus, the feel of him as Titus moved close to touch.

This was what he'd always wanted, what he needed, and Draven wasn't going to screw it up.

He had to trust in Titus, and in the love they'd both confessed to.

Draven looked like he had something serious on his mind. For some reason, that made Titus nervous. Draven wasn't likely to be planning on leaving him, but Titus didn't want to hear anything that might dim the joy of their shared admissions. He cupped Draven's chin and looked into his eyes. "Whatever it is that you're thinking about, can you let it go for tonight?"

"But it—"

"Just for tonight," Titus cut in, his heart hammering with a mix of anxiety and anticipation. "Unless you're going to admit to being someone—something—horrible, then it can wait. Please. I know you aren't a monster, so whatever it is that's weighing on your mind, it can't be as awful as you think it is. Tell me tomorrow. I'll listen, and I won't jump to any conclusions."

"Define horrible," Draven said, but his mouth curved up in a crooked smile.

Titus had to taste that grin. He leaned in and brushed his lips over Draven's.

Heat coiled in his belly and spread to his groin. He kissed Draven again, then again, licking into the warmth of his mouth. Draven's familiar flavor shot through Titus and his cock grew hard as he deepened the kiss. He moved his hand down, caressing Draven's neck, his shoulder, down his chest until Titus ran his knuckles over Draven's left nipple.

Draven moaned and shivered for him. Titus plucked at the stiffening tip as he sucked on Draven's tongue. Maybe he should have let Draven speak, but Titus needed this bonding with Draven.

He straddled Draven's lap and buried his other hand in Draven's hair, palming the back of Draven's head. Titus held him still as the kiss became rougher, as he pinched and tugged on Draven's nipple.

Draven began to squirm, not pulling away but pressing into the touches, thrusting his hips, gripping Titus' ass and kneading it.

Titus kept kissing him, kept teasing his nipple for another minute or so before he began nipping his way down Draven's neck, sucking up a mark here and there as he tasted Draven's skin in various places.

Draven's neck was saltier by his ear than the hollow of his throat. Licking Draven's collarbone made Draven gasp. Titus bit at the sensitive spot, then resumed his path down to the nipple he'd been playing with. He sealed his lips around it and sucked while pinching the other one.

Draven cursed and bucked. He shoved his hands down the back of Titus' shorts and pressed his fingers along Titus' crease.

It felt good, but Titus needed more of Draven.

Titus slid down until he was kneeling between Draven's legs. He mouthed the deep line dividing Draven's abs, licked his belly button and kept playing with Draven's nipples.

Titus left a purple mark on either side of Draven's belly button, then rubbed his cheek over the hot swell of Draven's shaft. A wet spot began to spread from where the tip of Draven's cock pressed against the cotton material.

Titus rumbled and took as much of Draven's thick cock into his mouth as he could with the shorts in the way.

Draven cried out and bucked. He settled his hands on Titus' head. "Please."

That raspy plea was one Titus couldn't resist. He rubbed his face all over the wet material, feeling the heat of Draven's cock through it before he unfastened Draven's shorts.

Draven's cock was right there for Titus to suck, and he did, even as he tugged, and Draven raised his butt enough for Titus to pull his shorts down. Titus didn't hesitate — he took Draven's length, let the thick head into his throat and swallowed as he palmed Draven's balls.

The sound Draven made was one of desperate need. Titus nodded enough for Draven to get the message. Draven tightened his hold on Titus' head and began to thrust.

Titus wanted to watch, and he did for a few seconds. Then his own need made itself achingly known. He freed his dick and fisted it, jacking his shaft as he let Draven take control of the blowjob, let Draven grunt and curse, let him fuck deep and rougher. Titus had never given to anyone what he gave to Draven — everything.

Draven cried out and his rhythm vanished. Hot cum pulsed down Titus' throat, and a second later, Titus came, his head spinning and body tensing before heat encompassed him. He lost himself in the pleasure, in what he felt, and what he'd given to Draven.

And later, when the last of his climax had faded away, and Draven was sleeping beside him after they'd stumbled to bed, Titus vowed that, no matter what Draven told him tomorrow, he'd stand by Draven's side.

Chapter Twenty-Five

The ringing of a phone woke Draven. He bit back a groan as he opened his eyes. It was too early to face the day—except it was still dark out. He sat up as Titus muttered in his sleep but didn't wake up. It was Titus' cell that was making a racket on Draven's nightstand. He'd plugged his phone and Titus' in after they'd made love. Seeing their phones side by side had made him feel sappier than he'd ever thought himself capable of being.

Draven grabbed Titus' phone and thumbed down the volume. He frowned at the lack of caller ID. It was probably a wrong number or some telemarketer from hell. Draven's gut clenched. *It could be Joel.*

Draven sat up just as the ringing stopped. The screen went dark. He set the phone down, telling himself not to be paranoid, not to borrow trouble.

The phone lit up again, before Draven's head even hit the pillow. His heart slammed against his ribs. He glanced at Titus, who still slept peacefully. Draven grabbed Titus' phone, slipped out of bed and rushed from the room. As soon as he was in the hall, he hit *Accept* and raised the phone to his ear. He didn't speak. If Joel were the caller, the last thing Draven wanted to do was anger him by letting him hear a man other than Titus answering Titus' phone.

Draven heard nothing other than the rush of his own pulse. He tried to will himself to calm down. Taking a few deep breaths would have helped but he didn't want to risk making any noise.

It didn't matter. A dial tone sounded a moment later. Draven sucked in a sharp breath — and the phone lit up with a call again. No caller ID was available. His gut clenched as he let it ring a second, then third time before he hit *Accept* once more.

This time the silence sent chills down his spine. It went on for over a minute, then the call was disconnected — and the phone lit up again.

Draven held down the power button and shut the phone off. His palms were sweaty from a mix of nerves and heat. He'd opened the bedroom windows so the breeze could blow through the screens, but the rest of his place was locked up.

He needed to go close those windows. Panic spiked as he darted back into the bedroom to take care of that. He paused at the foot of the bed to study Titus, who slept on unaware of Draven's fears that Joel was behind the calls. Draven knew he could be wrong, that the calls could have nothing to do with Joel or even Titus.

But he didn't believe in coincidence, and he certainly wouldn't risk Titus' life on the chance that the calls were accidents.

Draven watched the steady rise and fall of Titus' chest. The need to touch Titus, to hold him and assure himself that Titus was safe, was almost overpowering.

Keeping Titus safe was paramount. Draven walked over to the windows and closed them. He made sure no one was lingering around outside—his night vision was spot-on and there weren't any good hiding places for someone to utilize.

If it was Joel calling, he can't possibly know where Titus is, and I am going to go with the calls having been made by Joel. It's better to be cautious. Especially with the life of the man he loved.

Draven closed the curtains over the windows, something he hardly ever did. The moonlight and stars always soothed him when he looked out at them. Tonight, that wasn't the case.

He left the room again, then went around to every window and both doors leading outside, making certain they were all locked up tight. He peered out toward the ocean and saw nothing moving on the beach save the skittering crabs.

Titus was safe. Joel wasn't there. Draven looked down at the phone he still held in his hand. There was no doubt that he'd tell Titus about the calls. As much as Draven would hate to worry him, it was necessary. Titus had every right to know, too. Draven respected him and treating him like he was incapable of dealing with the potential of danger would be an insult at the very least.

Draven had planned to tell Titus about who and what he was in the morning. Now he wondered if he should wait, not for his own sake, but for Titus'.

Draven made his way back to where Titus was sleeping. He'd tell Titus about the calls first and depending on how Titus seemed to feel after that—if he was concerned, very worried, or whatever else he might feel—Draven would bare his soul.

Chapter Twenty-Six

Titus woke to the sensation of being watched. He didn't panic. He knew Draven's stare, recognized the way his own body went warm with desire. Titus opened one eye, didn't see Draven and opened the other. He propped himself up on his elbows, blinking as he turned his head and found Draven standing in the doorway.

"Sorry," Draven said in a quiet voice. "Didn't mean to creep you out."

"You didn't," Titus assured him. *Does he look like there's something wrong?* Titus' stomach dropped. *Oh. He has something to tell me that he thinks I won't like.* "It's okay, whatever it is," Titus said as he sat up fully, the sheet pooling in his lap. "Come in and sit by me. Talk to me."

Draven took a step, and Titus saw it then, his phone in Draven's hand. "Did I have a call or something?"

Draven closed the distance between them and sat beside him. "Both. Your phone started ringing in the middle of the night. No caller ID."

Titus felt the panic begin to form in his core. "Oh? Did you...?" He gulped. "Did you answer it?" *If it had been Joel, and he heard another man's voice...* "I changed my number, but I'm easy to find. Wanted to be, for the parents and..." Titus' throat tightened, and he glanced down at his hands.

"I didn't speak, but neither did whoever was calling. I didn't want to wake you up. I should have, instead of answering the phone. Well, sort of answering it." Draven tossed the phone down by Titus' hip. "Maybe it was nothing. I haven't turned it back on to see if there are messages or anything."

Titus nodded. He didn't reach for the phone but stared at it like it was a poisonous snake in his midst.

"Do you want me to check the phone?" Draven asked.

Titus took a stuttering breath. "No, I should. I — I'm acting like an idiot."

Draven placed his hands over Titus' and waited until Titus looked him in the eyes to continue. "You are not. Your ex was a violent, dangerous man, and I doubt he's changed any. He's probably not going to leave you alone so easily."

Titus' eyes burned. "Why not? Why wouldn't he say screw it, and leave me alone? He fucking went to prison for what he did!"

Draven pulled Titus right into his arms. "People like him don't care. Now, maybe I'm wrong. Might not be him at all. He could have learned something in there, for all I know. I just — I think being prepared is wise."

Titus nodded, his cheek rubbing against Draven's warm chest. "It is. He can't find me here, but it would be easy enough for him to track down where I teach and live."

Draven scooped the phone up with one hand. "Well, let's turn this on, then we can call Stacy and Michelle."

"Yeah, we need to call them. They're already aware of the situation and are keeping an eye out on my place. Stacy even found Joel's mugshot, so she knows what he looks like." Titus laughed shakily. "She also stalked his family online, so she has all their social media information and pics of Joel."

"You have amazing friends." Draven kissed Titus' cheek, then turned the phone on. He held it to where Titus could see it when all the missed calls and voicemail notices came on. "Damn it," Draven growled.

Titus took the phone from him. "He used to do this, you know. Call me non-stop if I didn't answer right away. I'd get back from a visit with my folks or from a class, or even the grocery store, and I'd have dozens of calls. He never would leave a message, though. Later on, he said he wasn't stupid enough to leave evidence." Titus hand trembled and he almost dropped the phone.

"Fucker," Draven snarled. "I'll tear him to pieces and feed him to the sharks. I know some — "

Titus waited for him to continue since it seemed an odd place to stop talking, but after several seconds, it became clear that Draven wasn't going to finish what he'd been saying.

Rather than push, and not taking Draven's threat seriously, Titus forced himself to look at all the missed calls. Every one of them lacked a number and caller ID. He played the voicemails, at least the first few. "Nothing but silence."

"Do you think it's him?"

Titus began deleting the calls and voicemails. "I can't prove it, but I think it's best to believe it is. Better safe than sorry." *Or dead. He'll kill me if he can.*

Draven stiffened and tipped Titus' chin up so that Titus looked at him. "How dangerous is he?"

"It's like you read my mind," Titus murmured before he could think better of it.

Draven's expression darkened. "He's not getting near you."

Titus wished he could believe that, but he knew Joel, knew his anger, his determination, *his fists and boots and* —

Draven kissed him, a gentle brush of lips that snapped Titus out of his rapidly building fear. Titus moved closer, pressing as close to Draven as he could. As much as Draven wanted to, he wouldn't be able to protect Titus from Joel, not all the time. Titus would have to go back to work, return home, and if Joel was looking for him, he'd find him.

Draven slipped his hand back to Titus' nape and deepened the kiss.

Titus let go of his worries and gave himself to Draven, needing him so much, nothing else mattering at the moment.

But Draven eased back and rubbed his nose against Titus', a little affectionate move that added to the love he felt for Draven.

"I have friends who will help watch for him," Draven said. "As much as I want to lay you down and make love with you, we need to discuss this, and…and I have to tell you something. About me."

Titus wanted to protest, but he could tell Draven needed to get whatever he wanted to confess off his chest. Rather than move away, however, Titus simply leaned his head against Draven' shoulder and said, "Tell me whatever it is. I don't believe for one second you've done something bad, so what is it?"

Draven huffed. "Not sure you'll believe me. It's going to sound crazy. I'm not. It's not."

Titus kissed his neck. "I trust you. Tell me, then we can make love, *then* deal with everything else."

"You might not want me after I tell you."

Titus sat up then. He studied Draven. "What could you possibly tell me that would make me not want you? Are you a…Republican?"

Draven didn't even grin at the joke. "No. I'm a shifter."

Titus shook his head. Those words did not compute. "What? You—what?" All he could think about were werewolves and things like that, things that didn't exist.

"I'm a manta ray shifter. So is Riveen. He was messing with you the other day."

Titus scrambled out of bed, but he didn't run off. "I'm not running away. Just…er. Shifters don't exist." How could Draven be delusional, and how did Titus miss it?

Draven looked incredibly sad as he lowered his head. "We do. We always have. My—I had one serious lover, and he threatened to expose us. Secrecy is the only reason we aren't extinct. And now I've told you, because I love you and want to be honest with you. I have no reason to lie."

He didn't, but that didn't mean he was a shifter. Somehow, Titus couldn't bring himself to call Draven a liar or ask if he needed psychiatric care.

And he thought of the manta ray in the water, the way it had acted so…*aware*.

Titus began to shiver so hard that his teeth chattered. Things were coming together in his mind—the way Draven seemed to need water, the scent of him, the—well, Titus didn't have a long list, but his brain was doing calculations and telling his logical side to fuck off.

"I can show you," Draven rasped, tilting his head just enough to glance at Titus. "Outside. In the water."

Titus didn't know what to say. He'd either get confirmation that Draven was delusional, or that he was something...spectacular. *Or maybe I'm the one who's hallucinating.*

"Are you going to leave me?"

Titus jolted like he'd been shocked. "Leave you?" *Will I, if any of these scenarios are true? Maybe if I'm the one who is delusional.*

Draven's breath hitched and he turned his head away. "I have never loved anyone as I love you, but if this is too much, I'll understand."

It was impossible. It had to be. And yet, Titus found himself growing calmer with each passing second. He loved Draven. Draven had been nothing but amazing with him. *How could Draven have hidden that he hallucinated or...or whatever?* Titus didn't see how he could have, not in as much time as they'd spent together.

"You were so scared of Rive, when he was—" Draven flapped his arms slowly. "Shifted."

For some reason, that gesture eased Titus' fears over the matter, at least a little. "He was still an asshole," Titus pointed out.

Draven snapped his head up so fast that Titus was afraid he'd hurt himself. "You believe me?"

Titus bit his bottom lip and gave a curt nod. "Either that, or I'm losing it."

Draven got up and held one hand out to Titus. "You aren't. Come with me."

Despite thinking he should be freaking out, Titus was just…calm — partially because he was still trying to wrap his mind around Draven's revelation.

They walked hand in hand to the edge of the water. Draven exhaled and glanced at him. "It's easier if I'm in the water, hidden. Under the pier is where I usually shift. That way, if anyone happens to be watching me, they don't think I dived underwater and drowned."

Titus shook his head, not to negate Draven's words, but to help them sink in and become reality. "They just think you never came out from under the pier?"

"Or I went down the beach that way," Draven pointed. "It curves right after the pier."

"Yeah." Titus knew that. He just wasn't thinking clearly. His nerves tingled almost painfully as the water lapped at his toes.

Draven let go of his hand and instead caressed his cheek. "I don't have to do this now. It's enough that I told you, and you didn't leave me."

Titus frowned at Draven. "Leave you? I told you, I love you. That means something to me."

"You said that before I admitted what I am," Draven replied. "I would understand if you changed your mind now. Or after you see me shift."

Titus was insulted. "I'm not that flighty!"

"It's not being flighty to freak out when you find out your lover isn't exactly human," Draven said.

"You're human," Titus argued, scowling. "Just, human and more."

Draven surprised him with a laugh. "Okay. Okay. You win. Want to come in the water with me?"

Titus nodded. "I want to see you…shift."

Draven took his hand again and tugged.

They didn't get more than a foot deep before a manta ray came toward them.

"Asshole," Draven muttered. "He's just trying to show me up."

Titus forced himself not to hesitate as they approached the manta ray. "Is that Riveen?"

"Yes."

Titus stopped by the creature and squatted. His hand shook despite his best effort not to let that happen. "Riveen, are you being a showoff?" Titus poked the ray right on top of the head. Its skin was soft and warm. *His. Riveen's. Not it.* Titus added a nudge, pushing Riveen down a little. "Stop tormenting your brother. I love him, you know."

Draven pulled Titus up and kissed him, driving out all thoughts and worries with the press of warm lips and the glide of his tongue.

In that moment, there was only Draven, and sunlight, a gentle breeze, and warm water. Titus could have stayed there forever, frozen time and kept that small piece of it for them. But a seagull dive-bombed them, and Draven jerked back, cursing and flapping his hands at the bird.

"Maybe it thought your hair was breakfast?" Titus asked.

Draven scowled. "No, that's not a regular seagull. That's my cousin, Ennis."

"Your…" Titus watched the seagull dive toward them again.

It was quite amazing to see a manta ray leap from the water.

Titus stumbled back along with Draven, the seagull squawked and shat on Riveen, and Titus burst out laughing at the weird whistle-rumble Riveen loosed. The seagull dived at Riveen.

"Run," Draven advised, nudging Titus.

Titus made for the pier with Draven beside him. By the time they reached it and turned around, the seagull was gone, and Riveen was somewhere in the water.

"How can you have a cousin that's a seagull?" Titus asked, unable to censor himself.

Draven shrugged. "Well, one of his parents is a seagull shifter. One's a good creature, a manta ray."

"Oh. So the…offspring is one or the other?"

"Yeah."

Titus glanced back at the sky. "And seagulls are inferior?"

Draven snickered. "Only when we're insulting each other."

"Family rivalry?" Titus smiled as he turned back to Draven. "Better watch that. The gulls have good aim."

"They do, but they can't swim like we can." Draven took a deep breath. "Are you ready?"

"Want me to hold your shorts?" Titus replied. He held out his hand.

Draven slipped his trunks off and gave them to Titus. "If you really don't freak out, I'd love to bring you back out here tonight and swim with you as a ray."

"That sounds amazing, actually." Titus was still waiting to freak out, but he felt less and less like that was going to happen. Actually, he was…*happy. Amazed. Life is so much more than I thought it was!*

Draven kissed him quickly, then dropped down into the water. Titus watched as he went from being a very sexy man one second then a manta ray the next. A second ray swam up, but Titus barely paid Riveen any attention, couldn't when Draven was so glorious, his wingspan incredible, his coloring more vibrant than Riveen's. "You are beautiful," Titus murmured, reaching down and stroking Draven. "Amazing. The most amazing manta ray ever."

He got splashed for that, of course. "Asshole," Titus muttered to Riveen, wiping saltwater from his eyes. "You're just jealous because Draven's handsomer than you in both forms!" He was teasing, for the most part, though Titus believed it to be true.

Draven smacked Riveen, then glided through the water, circling Titus slowly.

Titus laughed. And laughed. Joy spilled from him, and he couldn't remember when he'd felt so happy, so young and carefree.

Joel was out of prison, someone was making calls to Titus' phone, and his boyfriend wasn't entirely human—and there had never been a better moment in Titus' life before then.

Chapter Twenty-Seven

Draven tried to be careful, but he just had to play with Titus in the water for a little while. Riveen went off to torment someone else, and Draven had Titus all to himself.

Titus stared at him with wonder, a slight smile curving his mouth up on one side. He petted Draven all over as Draven swam around him. When Titus found Draven's itchy spot—the place just down on the left side of his back—Draven would have purred if he could have managed it.

As amazing as it felt to be with Titus like this, Draven knew he needed to shift back. He let Titus caress him one more time, then glided to the beam that supplied the most cover. He shifted and stood, but before he could reach for his shorts, Titus pulled him in for a kiss that made Draven's toes curl.

It wasn't just his toes affected by the kiss, either, but it was broad daylight now and there'd be no sex under the pier. With a grumble when Titus ended the kiss, Draven took his shorts and put them on.

"You're incredible," Titus said. "I'm just — wow."

"I'm just me," Draven countered, aware of the blush heating his face. "You're the incredible one."

Titus' smile could have lit up a pitch-black room. "We'll just have to agree to be each other's biggest fan."

Draven winked at him and was delighted when Titus blushed, too. "Definitely already yours."

Titus nudged his groin against Draven's. "Think you can come back to your place and show me? That whole 'actions speak louder than words-thing' comes to mind."

"Bet on it." Draven grinned, wondering if he looked as predatory as he felt.

Titus licked his lips, then licked Draven's.

Then Titus spun around and made a mad dash for the shore, which never worked well as deep as they'd been. Three or four steps out, a wave or the shifting sand of the ocean floor — or both — took Titus down.

He popped back up sputtering and laughing, and Draven froze, in awe of the joy he saw in Titus' expression, in awe of the man himself. *How did I get so lucky?*

Titus swiped the water off his face and laughed again. He didn't speak, but he didn't have to. There was no missing the love in his gaze as he held his hand out to Draven.

Draven took Titus' hand in his. "What do you want to do today?"

Titus squeezed his hand gently. "Oh, I don't know. I'd kind of like to get out for a while, go to some of the non-touristy spots in town. Walk around, have lunch, maybe see a movie before we come home and make love all night long. Guess dinner should be in there somewhere."

"We could start with making love," Draven countered, "Then go out. There's a local arts and craft show going on in Corpus, I think."

"Anticipation is a good thing," Titus said, giving Draven a smoldering look. "I want you to spend the day out with me, thinking about how I'm going to blow your mind when we get back tonight."

Draven's cock reacted predictably, plumping up as he walked beside Titus. "Oh? What do you have planned, exactly?"

Titus shook his head. "Nope. I want you to wonder about it. Remember, anticipation. It's a thing."

Draven groaned. "It's a thing that might kill me, but for you, I'll do anything."

In truth, he was more turned on by Titus' plan than he'd have ever thought he'd be.

They jogged up the steps to the house, and Draven held the door open for Titus.

"Shower with me?" Titus asked.

Draven groaned, although he was teasing for the most part. "But we can't get each other off?"

"We can—" Titus began, only to stop when his cell phone began to ring. "That's Stacy's ringtone. She doesn't call me often—it's usually Michelle."

He looked worried as he rushed to get his phone. Draven followed, concern pressing down on him. He didn't know why, but he felt bad news was coming with the call.

"Hey, Stacy, you're on speaker. What's up?" Titus asked. Draven didn't miss the nervous pitch to his voice. "Is everyone okay?"

"As far as I know, yeah," Stacy said. "Michelle would have called, but she's talking to the police. Someone broke into your place last night or early this morning. I don't know the extent of the damage done, but Michelle said some hateful things had been painted on some of the walls inside. I think the police might want to talk to you. They'll have to know."

Titus closed his eyes. "Yeah, they will, then everyone in town will know. I can kiss my job goodbye."

"Maybe not. Maybe we're all too worried about something that wouldn't happen if we came out." Stacy sighed. "Maybe we should think about whether or not we want to live the rest of our lives hiding that we love who we love. We can have this discussion another time. You need to come back."

"I know." Titus looked defeated, his happy glow gone, his shoulders rounded. "And whatever happens with my job happens. I'll be there as soon as possible."

"*We'll* be there." Draven cupped Titus' cheek.

Titus nodded. "We'll be there." He ended the call and turned to Draven, wrapping his arms around Draven's waist.

Draven hugged him tightly. He didn't want to scare Titus, but if Joel were the one who'd broken in—and he almost certainly was—then he could very well be hiding out somewhere around town, waiting. Watching.

In fact, Draven would bet on that being the case. Joel had broken in, knowing Titus would be called home because of it.

"It could be someone else," Titus murmured.

"Do you think it is?" Draven asked.

Titus shuddered. "No."

"Trust your gut."

"I trust you," Titus whispered. "I love you."

"He won't touch you," Draven vowed. "Not one hair on your head." Draven would do whatever he had to do to keep his word.

Chapter Twenty-Eight

Titus' palms were clammy, and he was sweating — not abnormal reactions to a south Texas summer, but he was sitting in an air-conditioned lobby of the police department waiting to be called into Deputy Martinez's office. Titus couldn't sit still. He twiddled his fingers and jostled one leg, bouncing his foot.

Draven touched his hand but kept the contact brief. "It'll be okay. I know it doesn't seem like it now, and…and things may change, but in the end, it *will* be okay."

Titus wished he could believe that. "Maybe we should have gone by the house first. I know Martinez said to meet him here, but —"

"Mr. Eisenhower?"

Titus and Draven stood and looked at the man — the deputy — saying his name. "Deputy Martinez?" He saw the deputy's name tag and blushed. *I'm an idiot.* "Sorry."

Draven grunted. "You have nothing to apologize about."

Deputy Martinez gave them a half-smile and nodded. "That's correct, Mr. Eisenhower. You've got to be shaken up. If you and…"

"My boyfriend," Titus blurted out, then realized Martinez had probably been expecting a name, not a relationship update.

"Draven Costille," Draven added.

Martinez nodded. "If y'all would step into my office so we can speak in private?"

"Of course, and please, call me Titus." Titus wished he could hold Draven's hand for support, could lean on him like any straight couple would have been free to do, but he had spent years being cautious. It was ingrained in him, and he resented that.

"Sure." Martinez held the door open for them then shut it once they'd entered. He walked around and sat behind his desk.

Titus and Draven took the seats across from him.

"Titus," Martinez began, leaning forward and bracing his forearms on the desk. "I want to make it clear that I don't care about your sexuality, that you have a boyfriend, any of that. I'm here to do a job. I took an oath to serve and protect, and there are no exceptions to that. I work for you and for everyone with the same integrity and determination."

Titus exhaled a little shakily. "Thank you. That's — just, thank you."

Martinez gave him that hint of a smile. "You don't have to thank me for doing my job. I'm sorry that was ever a concern, but I *do* get it. Now." He sat back again, then picked up a file. "I have pictures of the crime scene. There are three specific threats painted on the walls, and another four slurs." He opened the file and glanced at Draven.

Something seemed to pass between them. Draven took Titus' hand and held it between both of his.

"I believed this was a personal attack because of the three threats." Martinez slid out several photos. "I know this is frightening, but I, and the rest of the department, will do everything we can to keep you safe." He passed the pictures over.

Titus bit his bottom lip as he moved the images around so he could see them. The first one made him feel like he was going to puke. It was a threat to commit a specific sexual act on Titus, along with smaller script stating, 'I know just how you like to bleed'.

"Son of a bitch," Draven growled. He moved one hand up then put his arm around Titus' shoulders. "No way this fucker's getting near you."

The other photos were just as bad. Titus heard a buzzing in his ears and his vision dimmed.

"Breathe, baby," he heard Draven say, though he sounded far off.

Then Titus was being moved, his legs parted and his head being tucked down between them.

"He's not gonna win," Draven said. "We won't let him."

"I need to know who *he* is," Martinez said. "Or if it's who I believe it to be. Joel—"

"No, no, no," Titus rasped, pressing his hands over his ears. "I can't. I can't. I thought I could but I can't."

Whatever Draven said, Titus didn't hear. He closed his eyes and focused on trying to breath, then on pushing the panic back until his heart didn't feel like it was going to burst out of his chest.

Slowly, he became aware of Draven's voice, low and calm, of his big hand rubbing soothing circles on Titus' back. He didn't rush Titus or make any demands. After several minutes, Titus stopped shaking and the buzzing in his head began to fade. His chest ached like he'd been holding his breath too long, but he knew that was from breathing erratically. He went hot with embarrassment and wanted to just disappear, but Draven's quiet reassurances finally helped Titus to sit up and, while he couldn't meet Martinez's eyes, he at least got his gaze level with the surface of the desk.

Every few seconds, Titus would jerk as he tried to settle. The photos were gone, and he was grateful for that at least, but he didn't think he could take much more humiliation, especially not by his body and brain freaking out on him.

"I'd like to tell you why I became a police officer," Martinez said after a moment. "It's not something I share often or want to think about. I still have nightmares and see a therapist because of it."

Titus finally managed to look at the deputy.

Martinez tipped his head to the left and touched his neck, back by his hairline. "My brother was six years older than me. He was a gangbanger in SA. He terrorized my parents and me from the time he was fifteen on. Lots of people don't understand how a kid could rule a household, but those people didn't live it. Jaime had a history of violence, but my folks didn't want people to know about the pets he killed or the cruel threats he made. That would have brought shame on our family. Instead, they lived in fear and so did I. Jaime hurt all of us."

He touched the spot. "This is from the last time, when he was going to shoot me in the head. If he had hit where he'd been aiming, I'd have been killed. He'd already murdered our parents in a fit of rage. I was twelve when I was shot. I don't remember much after that. When I woke up, I was in the hospital, and everything came rushing back to me. I tried to tear out my IV. I didn't want Jaime to find me. There was no calming me down except with a shot of tranquilizer than knocked me out. It happened again, then a third time, and I probably would have lost my mind if it hadn't been for one cop, the man who inspired me to be who I am today, agreed to show me that Jaime was dead. Now, I know Jaime is dead, but he's still here." Martinez tapped his temple. "He still haunts me and terrifies me sometimes, so I *do* understand, Titus. And there's no shame in that fear, in what was done to you. The shame is on him, on the person who would and does hurt others for fun or whatever twisted reasoning they come up with."

"I'm sorry," Titus rasped. "For what happened to you."

Martinez inclined his head. "Thank you. I'm sorry, too. For me, for you, for everyone who is a victim. But your boyfriend is right. We're not going to let the man who hurt you win."

Titus stared at Martinez, then turned to Draven.

Draven pulled him into a hug that ended up with Titus on his lap.

"I want to go home," Titus murmured. "After we finish here, I want to go home."

"Your house will need to be—"

Titus shook his head at Draven. "No. Home. With you." He needed that and needed to be away from the words that had desecrated the house he'd lived in for years. He stood. "Thank you, Deputy Martinez. I'm sorry I fell apart."

Martinez shook his head. "Don't be sorry. I told you, I still have nightmares and bad moments. You've got to learn to let go of the guilt. That's the hardest part, sometimes. Forgiving ourselves for not being the epitome of machismo society tells us to be."

The truth in that statement hit Titus in the chest. He took a half-step back and nodded. "Yes, you're right."

"I'll contact you when I have something more to tell you. We won't get the fingerprint results back for weeks. If this were a TV show, I'd already have them along with hair follicles, footprints and a convenient neighbor who decided to come forward and tell me he or she saw it all." Martinez walked past them and opened the door for them. "Unfortunately, reality is a lot slower."

"I understand." Titus itched to be out of town, back in the safety of Draven's home. He was growing calmer by the minute, but the need for his lover was not diminished.

After a few more words with the deputy, Titus and Draven finally left the police station.

Titus hesitated on the sidewalk and glanced around. A few people were out and about, but no one seemed to be paying him and Draven any mind.

"What's wrong?" Draven asked, touching his lower back briefly.

"Nothing. Just...thinking." Titus looked at him. "This really isn't home to me. All those romantic stories about home being found in someone, not in a place — they're all right. I love my job, but I'd love teaching anywhere."

Draven smiled tentatively. "Are you hinting that I should ask you to move in with me, permanently?"

Was he? Titus pursed his lips. Had he been hinting? "No, I think I was being more obvious than hinting. I want to live with you, and I can probably find a job teaching somewhere not too far from...from home."

Draven's smile broadened. "I'd love that. Will—?"

"Titus!"

Titus ignored Stacy and Michelle calling his name. "Will I what?" His heart raced. "What were you going to ask?"

Draven sighed. "Another time."

"But—" Titus closed his mouth. Stacy and Michelle were less than a dozen feet away. Whatever Draven had been about to ask—if it were what Titus hoped he was going to ask—Titus would prefer it to be done in private.

On the beach as the sun is setting... But I don't have to wait for him to ask. I could ask—

"Titus, I'm sorry." Stacy hugged him. "Michelle and I will repaint the walls once we can get into the place. Let us do that for you."

Titus hugged her back and met Michelle's gaze over Stacy's shoulder. "I think you should know, I'm probably not going to stay there. Here."

Stacy hugged him tighter. "That's okay. We're still going to clean up your house and paint the walls, do what we can to help. Whether you live here or not, you're my best friend, Titus, and I love you. Michelle and I will do anything we can to help you. That's not dependent on you living in this town and working at the school here."

A burden Titus hadn't known he was carrying lifted off his shoulders. "Thank you. That... You are..." He gave up trying to explain and just held on for the hug.

Eventually, he and Stacy separated. "Are you heading back?" Stacy asked. "I'd invite you to our place, but until this is settled, I think staying away from here is the wisest choice for you."

Titus knew he was blessed when it came to friends. "Yes, we're heading back. I can't be here right now."

Stacy hugged him again, this time a quick moment of contact before she stepped back. She turned to Draven. "Keep him safe."

"Always." Draven touched Titus' back again, but this time he kept his hand there. "You are welcome to come over any time. I have a guest room you can stay in, and the beach is right out through the back door."

Stacy hugged Draven, too. "You made the offer, and we're going to accept. Thank you."

"You're welcome," Draven replied.

"Be safe," Michelle said. She hugged them each.

Then Titus was walking to the car with Draven beside him, hand still resting on Titus' lower back.

It felt like a goodbye, not to his friends, but to the town itself. The roots he'd started to grow here had been hacked off and the ground thoroughly salted.

He should have felt sad, but all he experienced was relief as he watched the sign for the town grow smaller in the rearview mirror.

"The farther we get from there, the better I feel," he said to Draven. "Free. I feel free. Whatever I do next, wherever I work, I'm not hiding who I am, or who I love."

"Good," Draven replied. "I want to be able to bring you lunches and hold your hand while we're out in public. Not all the time, because I think you're as reticent there as I am, but…I want to get past that."

"So do I," Titus admitted. "We shouldn't have to be afraid."

"We shouldn't, and we won't be." Draven slid one hand up Titus' thigh, stopping with his fingers just centimeters from Titus' balls. "And when I get you home, I'm going to make love to you all night long." He moved his hand that little bit more, and caressed Titus' balls through his jeans.

"Sounds like the best idea ever," Titus scraped out, his throat dry as need began to coil in his gut. *The drive back is going to take forever.*

Chapter Twenty-Nine

"Oomph!" Draven barely had time to close the door before Titus was on him.

He flushed with need as Titus pushed him against the door and kissed him. There was nothing gentle or timid about the kiss. Titus was owning him, claiming him, and Draven's insides quivered with excitement.

Everything I ever wanted, and never thought I'd have. It was his last coherent thought before Titus blew his mind, sliding down Draven's body, licking, kissing, nibbling, leaving marks after he shoved Draven's shirt up.

"Want you," Titus mumbled as he began to unfasten Draven's pants. "Need you."

Draven tried to agree, but Titus mouthed his cock through the denim, and Draven's eyes rolled back as he moaned. He buried his fingers in Titus' hair, more for support than guidance.

Titus hummed, and Draven's legs trembled. Chances were good he wasn't going to remain upright for long.

When Titus shoved Draven's pants and briefs down, then licked over his leaking tip, Draven cried out. He started to slide down, then the world tipped and Draven was utterly confused. By the time he figured out that Titus had hoisted him into a fireman's carry, Draven was being flopped onto the bed.

Then Titus was back on him, nearly ripping Draven's shirt off. Draven couldn't keep up. His head was spinning with the force of his need. He tried to help get his clothes off, and whether he did, or whether he hindered Titus' efforts, he couldn't have said.

But he was naked, and Titus was kissing him, and nothing else mattered. Draven touched Titus everywhere he could reach. He fed off the warmth and strength of his lover, off the desire they shared.

Titus tugged on Draven's bottom lip, having caught it between his teeth. The sting went right to Draven's cock, and he thrust his hips, grinding against Titus, desperate to get more of him.

Titus released Draven's lip and began nipping his way down Draven's body once more. He loved on Draven's nipples, sucking and pinching them until Draven clawed at the bedsheets. "Please," he rasped, the word finally forming and escaping past his dry lips.

"Please…suck you?" Titus asked.

Draven spread his legs and tried to get his knees up to his chest. He couldn't speak, but he had no shame in showing Titus what he needed.

Titus scooted down, then his hot, wet mouth was on Draven's cock. Draven cried out and clutched at his knees. Titus showed him no mercy, palming his balls and tugging them gently while he took Draven's shaft in completely.

The pleasure enveloped everything. Draven was helpless to do anything other than *feel* as Titus sucked his cock. Only the grasp Titus had on Draven's balls kept him from coming.

Then Titus pulled off and flipped Draven over. Draven was still lost in pleasure, still had it thrumming through his system.

Titus pulled him to his knees, then pressed Draven's head down. He spread Draven's cheeks and licked over his hole.

Draven had been lust-dazed before, but it was nothing like where he went and what he felt as Titus rimmed him. Titus fucked him with his tongue until Draven was babbling nonsense, then used his fingers to open Draven up.

And finally, Titus slipped his cock into Draven with a slow, steady grind that set Draven's nerve endings on fire with need.

Titus bucked his hips once he was fully sheathed, then did it again, dragging a ragged moan out of Draven when Titus' dick rubbed over his gland.

"Draven," Titus muttered, then pulled out and slammed back in.

Draven shouted and dug his elbows into the bed, giving himself leverage so he could shove his ass back. The sound of his flesh and Titus' meeting echoed in the room and their panted breaths grew louder and more erratic as the fucking became more intense.

Draven's cock ached and his balls were drawn up tight. Titus reached under him and fisted his shaft. One squeeze of Draven's glans, and his orgasm tore through him.

"Draven!" He heard his name as if at a distance, then Titus was draped over him, shuddering, gasping.

Several minutes passed, then Titus rolled off him, whimpering as he flopped down beside Draven.

Draven forced his heavy eyelids open and turned on his side to look at Titus.

Titus was frowning at him.

Draven wasn't as sleepy as he'd been a second ago. He propped his head up on one hand as he studied Titus. "What's wrong?"

Titus blushed and averted his gaze. "I—I shouldn't have been so rough. I shouldn't—"

"Oh, no, no you don't," Draven cut in, moving right over to lie halfway on Titus. "Don't you dare apologize for fucking me senseless. I felt nothing but pleasure and ecstasy, Titus. Nothing but sensational feelings—and yours. Why would you be sorry about that?"

Titus' blush had darkened but he looked at Draven once more. "I'm not. I've never been so…demanding, before."

Draven kissed him, then rubbed his nose against Titus'. "You can be as demanding as you want with my ass any time."

Titus grinned and wrapped his arms around Draven. "I need you, in so many ways. You make it possible for me to just…just be me. I'm not sure I know who that is, but with you, I'll find out."

"I can tell you that you're an incredible man, sexy and smart and a god in bed," Draven told him.

Titus snorted. "A god? Seriously?"

Draven nodded. "Would I lie?"

Titus laughed, then brought one hand around to cup Draven's cheek. "I'm scared," he whispered. "And I hate that he scares me."

Draven hated it, too. "It's understandable, Titus. There's nothing wrong with what you're feeling. We're going to keep you safe, though. Me, Rive, our friends. We won't let him touch you. I promise you."

Titus stared at him for several seconds, then he tugged Draven down the inch or so that separated them and kissed him.

Chapter Thirty

Draven tensed as the hairs on his nape seemed to stand on end. He turned casually in the aisle of the local grocery store, reaching for a can of something on the shelf. He wasn't paying attention to that, but rather trying to find the cause for his sudden unease.

Titus had been with him for almost a week. There'd been no more attacks on his home, but he'd had numerous phone calls from an unknown number. Titus had quit answering those calls after the second one, when no one spoke.

Things had been calm.

Now, Draven's survival instinct was alerting him to potential trouble. Draven always trusted his gut — ever since Andres had betrayed him. He'd ignored little and bigger twinges of unease he'd felt around Andres at times. Draven had vowed never to make that mistake again.

So he cut his focus to the left, trying to see if someone was watching him from that direction.

What he saw made him drop the can of food he'd picked up.

The stranger glanced at him but didn't really look at him before resuming his perusal of offerings on the shelf.

Draven pivoted toward the figure and knew his jaw was hanging open. He stared at the profile of the man down at the end of the aisle. Glossy black hair that hung in waves to just past his shoulders, a muscular build, biceps that had to be earned in a gym.

Draven closed his mouth as his heart pounded. The man wasn't looking at him, which was a good thing. Draven's head was a chaotic place as memories from his past swamped him. The stranger in the aisle looked — as if thinking of him had made him appear — like Andres.

Not possible. Andres died. I saw him. He died fifty years ago, and this can't be him.

But the nose was long and pointed, a slight bump at the bridge, just like Andres' nose. He had the same tall, sloped forehead, shadowed cheeks and angular chin.

Draven forced himself to look away. Andres was dead, without a doubt, and even if he *had* survived for five decades, he'd have aged. He'd been a human, after all.

But Draven had seen him bleed out in the ocean, had turned away when sharks began to feed off his corpse.

It wasn't Andres standing twelve feet away.

There's supposed to be a twin for everyone on this planet. Or maybe Andres had family he never told me about.

Draven couldn't remember what he'd wanted to get. His insides were heating with that sensation of danger, and alarms were sounding in his head that he needed to get out, *now*. Even his manta ray was urging him to leave.

He didn't understand why, but he'd listen. He forced his feet to move, put one foot in front of the other, and he walked past the Andres-doppelganger, trying to study him without being obvious.

The scent of blood and saltwater hit him when he was directly behind the man. There was also the odor of peppermint, Andres' favorite candy.

Draven's mind was fucking with him. He kept his steps steady until he was about to round the corner of the aisle.

"Draven."

Draven's heart ricocheted in his chest until he realized it was Titus who'd spoken.

"What's wrong? You look..." Titus took the hand basket from him.

"Leave it. Let's go." Draven felt that prickly awareness again. "Now."

Titus pressed his lips into a thin line which meant he wasn't happy with Draven, but he nodded. "Okay. Let's put this stuff up first. I'm not leaving it here for the clerks to put back."

Draven's skin itched with the need for him to get out of there, to get Titus out of there. "Just—there, the express line." He pointed to the cashier in lane three. "He's open."

Titus headed for the register, and Draven followed him. He glanced back over his shoulder and caught a glimpse of the not-Andres man going around the corner of the aisle.

The scent of him was still in Draven's nostrils.

It had to be his head fucking with him. He'd been thinking about Andres, then...

"Did you see that guy with the black hair?" he asked Titus as Titus set the hand basket on the conveyor belt.

Titus turned to him. "Which guy?"

"Never mind."

Titus frowned at him. "No, not never mind. What guy?"

Draven bit back a sigh. "He went down the aisle after the one I was on."

"Pay for the stuff." Titus darted around Draven.

"Wait, no!" Draven clutched at Titus' hand.

Titus' frown deepened into a scowl. "What's going on, Draven?"

"Your total is ten sixty-three," the cashier said.

Titus slipped out of Draven grasp. "Pay the man. I'll be right back."

"Titus—"

"Pay. I'm not going to do anything stupid, just taking a peek. You'll see me the whole time."

"Is there a problem, sir? Sirs?" the cashier asked. He seemed worried and sincere.

Draven grunted and took out his wallet. "No. No problem." He handed a twenty over.

"Okay, sir."

Draven kept an eye on Titus, who, true to his word, didn't walk very far, just enough to peek down the aisle.

By the time Draven had his change and the grocery bag in hand, Titus was back at his side.

Neither of them spoke until they were in the car.

"Did you see him?" Draven asked.

Titus shook his head. "There was no one down that aisle."

Draven started the car as he pondered that. "Could have gone down the next aisle."

Titus shrugged. "I didn't see anyone down that aisle except a pair of elderly ladies. Guess your mystery man could have been standing at the endcap."

"He's not my mystery man," Draven muttered. "He fucking looked like Andres. Identical to him."

Titus had been in the process of buckling his seatbelt, but he stopped and placed one hand on Draven's right forearm. "He's here?"

Draven shook his head. "No, he's dead. I saw him die, saw the sharks start to— he's dead. It just threw me to see someone who could be his twin. Andres would have aged over fifty years—he was human. It couldn't have been him. Had to be my mind playing tricks on me and my body's alert system overreacted."

Titus leaned across and kissed Draven. "We've been under a lot of stress. A *lot*. I don't think you're hallucinating, but it must have been someone who resembled Andres enough to trigger your senses. I do believe you saw someone. You were as pale as a ghost when I found you."

Pale as a ghost. For some reason, those words stuck a chord of fear in Draven.

"He looked just like Andres," Draven reiterated. "I know it wasn't him. It still fucked with me."

"That's understandable." Titus reached for his seatbelt again. "It would mess with anyone in that situation."

"Yeah. Just…weird." He wanted to get home, lock the doors and get under the covers with Titus and stay there until he felt safe again.

It was a ridiculous thing to be experiencing. There was no reason for fear to be clawing at his gut.

Draven put the car in reverse and glanced in the rearview mirror. He stomped on the brake when a figure walked behind the car. "There! Him, the guy behind us!"

Titus twisted around to the left, then to the right. "What guy? Where?" He pressed his head against the passenger window. "I don't — oh. Black hair, to his shoulders or so?"

Draven felt dizzy as he spotted the man via the rearview mirror. "That's him." He blinked, and the man was staring back at him. Everything inside Draven froze. He couldn't look away.

"Fuck this." Titus unbuckled and opened the car door.

Draven tore his gaze away from the rearview mirror and reached for Titus. "Titus — "

But Titus was out of the car, and Draven threw the gear into park and unfastened his seatbelt too. He opened the door and got out just in time to see Titus jump back and narrowly miss being hit by a car.

"*Titus!*" Draven ran to him and wrapped him in his arms. "Gods be damned, don't — I can't lose you!"

Titus hugged him back. "I wasn't watching where I was going. That was my fault. The guy is leaving now. Let me — "

"Let him go. He doesn't matter." Draven held Titus as tight as he dared. "You matter. Whoever that man is, or isn't, doesn't matter. You. Just you."

Chapter Thirty-One

"He looked identical to Andres." Draven shook his head as he peeled the label off his beer. "It was creepy as fuck."

Riveen looked from him to Titus. "And he was watching you, or Draven?"

Titus nodded, mouth pinched tight before he spoke. "He was. Standing in the parking lot, just staring at Draven. Even when I got out of the car and was going to approach him, the man never looked away from Draven. I wanted to go ask him what the hell his problem was." But Draven had stopped him and asked Titus to let it go.

Titus still thought he should have followed his instinct and confronted the man.

"Andres is dead," Riveen said. He took a long pull of his own beer then set the bottle down. "I saw him. I stayed to make sure of it."

Draven blanched. "You stayed and watched?"

Riveen nodded. "Yup. That fucker needed to be dead. No way he survived having his limbs…er. He's dead."

"Right. Dead." Draven sighed. "I know that. He was probably staring because I was acting weird. I tried not to, but he threw me off. And he smelled—"

"Smelled like what?" Titus prodded.

Draven shook his head. "It's crazy, just my mind playing tricks on me because of the resemblance. He smelled like…like blood and water and peppermint." He whispered the last word.

Titus saw that Draven's hands were shaking. He straddled Draven's thighs and took Draven's hands in his. Draven looked at him, and Titus caught the hint of fear in his expression.

"Whatever is happening, we'll get through it," Titus murmured before dipping his head and kissing Draven's lips. It was a chaste kiss, not that that fact kept Riveen from whistling and cat calling.

Titus brushed his lips over Draven's again, then nuzzled his cheek. "Your brother is as mature as a tween boy."

"Hey!" Riveen huffed.

Draven snickered and released Titus' hands, then wrapped his arms around Titus. "I think you're giving him too much credit."

"Assholes," Riveen said. "I was going to offer to buy dinner, but never mind. I'm ordering from Noodle Bowl and having it delivered. Your treat, bro."

Draven might have flipped Riveen off—Titus felt him move one hand, and Riveen barked out a laugh.

Titus wondered, though he didn't speak the words, if there was some way that Andres could have been reborn or stitched together, *something*. The way the man in the parking lot had been looking at Draven, that had *not* been curiosity. If Titus had to guess, he'd say he'd seen anger, lust, hate, and something else, something possessive and greedy in the man's expression. There'd been a palpable current of something otherworldly in the air.

But Draven didn't seem to have noticed, and Titus didn't want to weird him out, or come across as being dramatic — or worse.

He kept his mouth shut and as the evening moved on, the mood seemed to lighten. Titus thought the matter of Andres had been dropped until Draven was in the bathroom and Riveen scrambled over to sit by Titus on the couch.

"Tell me exactly what that fucker at the store looked like," Riveen demanded in a low voice, his eyes narrowed and anger all but sparking off him. "Hurry up, before Draven gets back!"

Titus didn't waste time arguing. He gave Riveen all the details he could in the time that Draven was out of the room.

Riveen darted back to his seat then leapt up when Draven returned. "So! I think I'm going to go, let you two lovebirds have some time alone. Thanks for the food." His smile didn't quite come across as sincere, and Titus saw that Draven was frowning at his brother.

"What's going on?" Draven asked, glancing back at Titus.

Titus shrugged. "I don't know."

Riveen sighed as if he were the most put-upon person in the world. "Nothing is going on except I'm horny and want to hit up the club."

"That smile of yours is as fake as that excuse," Draven muttered.

"Uh, no, it isn't," Riveen retorted, then frowned and rolled his eyes as he exhaled. "I mean, it isn't a fake excuse, and my smile…well okay. That might not have been full-on-beam, but I'm saving the genuine one for whichever handsome stud I decide to take home tonight."

"Riveen—"

Riveen flapped a hand at Draven. "Nope. I'm out of here, bro. You two have fun. Lots of dirty, sweaty, sexy fun."

"Bye," Titus said. He got up and followed Riveen to the door. He hoped for a moment to ask Riveen what the heck he was up to, but Riveen flashed that smile again and sprinted down the steps without giving Titus the chance to speak.

"Damn." Titus locked the door. He turned around and Draven stood. "What's going on?"

"That's what I want to know," Draven replied. "He's up to something."

"He asked me about the guy," Titus admitted. "While you were in the bathroom. Then he split right after."

"Definitely up to something." Draven walked past Titus and looked out of the window. "He walked here. Bet we can follow him without him noticing."

"Do you think he's going to do something dangerous?" Titus asked, grabbing the house keys off the entryway table.

Draven snorted and unlocked the door, then opened it. "This is Riveen we're talking about."

Titus followed Draven out the door and locked it. "What happened with Andres? I mean, how did Riveen see…um."

Draven cupped Titus' elbow as they started down the steps. "We had the big confrontation on one of the little islets to the south of here. Andres admitted he'd been trying to sell us out, that he'd suspected I was not entirely human. He pulled a gun on me. Riveen came flying out of the water and tackled Andres. I dove in, and Andres tried to shoot Riveen. I got the gun away from him. He had a knife and he knicked Riveen. I kind of lost it. Someone pulled me off Andres and he got caught in the riptide. Then the sharks came. Not shifters, just sharks. I couldn't get to Andres. I saw…so much blood. Andres yelled once, and that was all. A few of our cousins had been loitering nearby, waiting and watching. They held me back when I tried to get to Andres. Then they forced me away from the pier."

"You couldn't have saved him," Titus said.

Draven swiped his free hand over his face. "I don't know if I would have. If I'd been given the time to think it over and not act on instinct. Andres wanted to expose my kind, me, my family, to the world. Do you know what would have been done to us?"

Titus could only imagine, and it wasn't good. "But Riveen stayed behind and watched."

"He says so. I don't think he'd lie about that," Draven admitted.

"There was something unnatural about the man you said looked like Andres," Titus muttered. "I felt it. Is there any way he could still be alive?"

"Even if he was still alive, he'd be almost eighty," Draven responded. "Not young. He was human. He'd have aged."

Titus wondered if there were more supernatural beings in the world than even Draven knew about.

* * * *

"He's not going to the club," Draven muttered as he and Titus trailed behind Riveen. They'd followed him to his place, then waited across the street in the shadows until Riveen had come back outside. "He wouldn't be wearing all black if he was."

"He did dress more...flashy...when he was out dancing," Titus agreed, sliding his hand in Draven's. "That looks like a cat-burglar getup."

Draven's gut went cold. Riveen had proven himself to be the more dangerous of the two of them, despite all his joking and party lifestyle. It had been Riveen who'd watched as Andres had been ripped apart by the sharks. Whether or not he could have intervened, Draven would never ask. Riveen was his brother, and he loved him like only a sibling could. The devotion and loyalty were stronger than any differences they'd ever have.

"I can't see him," Titus whispered, squinting in the direction Riveen had gone.

Draven could see him. "He's heading back the way we came. Maybe he's going to turn off somewhere else." He and Titus slipped out of the shadows and began following Riveen.

Minutes later, Draven cursed as Riveen parked himself in the copse of palm trees across from Draven's home. "He's watching out for us."

"He thinks someone is coming for us," Titus pointed out. "Otherwise, he wouldn't be here. Who does he think is coming for us?"

Draven grunted because he honestly didn't know. Except, it couldn't be Andres. "Andres is dead."

"Is he?" Titus asked, turning to face Draven.

Draven frowned at him. "Yes, he is. Riveen wouldn't lie about that."

Titus shook his head. "I don't think he'd lie but...but what happens to a person after they die?"

Draven blinked. "What?"

"What happens to a person after they die?" Titus repeated. "I never thought much about it. I don't like thinking about death, but that guy stared at you like he wanted to do something to you. I'm not sure what. That isn't the way a stranger generally ogles someone. It was very...intense. I've been thinking about it. It was like he knew you."

Draven didn't know what happened to people when they died. He'd always just assumed they were dead and gone. Heaven and hell had never been real places to him. He shivered as he remembered the man in the parking lot. "He looked identical to Andres. Identical."

Titus bit his bottom lip then released it. "Could he have been something more than human?"

Titus' cheeks went ruddy when he asked the question.

Draven mulled it over. "I—I had a limited education," he finally said. "Limited environment. My kind didn't hang out with humans until the last century, not that I know of, anyway. Too many torch-bearing, pitchfork-wielding angry people about. For that matter, I don't know much about our own history."

"Would Riveen know anything?"

"I doubt it. We were taught together," Draven explained. "More about survival than anything else. Reading and writing were things we didn't learn until we were almost adults. Working in this world was never an issue. Sunken ships provided a lot of,

hmm…income stability over the centuries. That much I
do know."

"You two are loud enough to wake the dead."

Draven bit back a yelp of surprise. Titus didn't. They
both spun around to find Riveen snickering.

"Seriously, I heard you while we were heading back
here," Riveen said. "And, um, let me just point out, if
you were spying on me…you lost track of me, and here
I am — ta-da!"

Titus groaned softly and covered his face with his
hands. "I suck at this."

Riveen patted his back. "Don't feel bad. You *both*
suck at stalking."

Draven opened his mouth to argue, but Riveen was
right. Instead, he asked, "How much of our
conversation did you hear?"

Riveen shrugged. "A lot. I don't know much of
shifter history, either. We just were never taught it, and
maybe there's a reason for that."

Titus had lowered his hands. He looked at Riveen.
"Could Andres be back? Reincarnated? Or maybe he
wasn't strictly human? Or human at all?"

Another shrug. "I don't know. I mean, if he looks
exactly like Andres, and he was staring like y'all
said…" Riveen shook his head and folded his arms
over his chest. "That's not right. Something fucked up
is going on, and I'm worried, so I want to keep an eye
out, preferably without everyone and their mama
knowing I'm doing it, so, you know. If you two would
just…scoot along? Go have sex or something."

Draven shook his head. "No. I'm not letting you do
this alone."

"Yeah. This involves us," Titus said.

"But you both suck balls at surveillance. And I don't mean that in a good way. Can't you just help by being the bait?" Riveen asked.

"Bait?" Draven didn't like that at *all*. "No, we aren't going to be bait. I don't want Titus in danger."

"But I'm in danger anyway," Titus pointed out. "As evidenced by what happened to my house."

"Double danger," Riveen added, nodding. "From that psycho ex and from the revived-from-the-dead Andres."

"It can't be him," Draven protested even as his gut went colder.

"Stranger things…" Riveen trailed off with a scowl. "I don't know the rest of that saying, but the point is, we don't know everything. Why wouldn't there be other supernatural beings in the world besides shifters? Or how can we say, without a doubt, that reincarnation isn't a thing? I know one hundred percent that the Andres who betrayed you died. There was no chance he survived. If he's back, then, well, it stands to reason he is either a supernatural being or he was reincarnated and can either access his memories of past lives, or maybe you were just *really* familiar to him."

"Fuck." Draven didn't know what to think. "I—"

A loud popping sound distracted him, and he glanced toward it.

Titus gasped. "Your house is on fire!"

Chapter Thirty-Two

Huddled with Draven on the couch at Riveen's place, Titus wrestled with the anger pressing down on him. Draven had finally fallen into a fitful sleep, and Titus didn't want to wake him, not even long enough to get him into the bed in the guest room. Draven had been — understandably — distressed over the loss of his home. Almost twenty-four hours later, he was getting the first sleep he'd had in days.

Titus wasn't able to join him in that possibly blissful escape. Someone had torched Draven's home. By the time he, Draven and Riveen had crossed the street, the entire property had been engulfed in flames. Even the staircases had been burning, and once the fire department had done what they could, nothing much was left besides ashes, melted lumps of appliances and a few torched beams.

That it had been arson surprised no one.

Titus' first inclination had been to think Joel had found him, but after the weirdness of the maybe-Andres thing, he wasn't certain at all that Joel had been the arsonist. A call to Deputy Martinez hadn't helped Titus to decide one way or the other about who might have started the fire.

That worry had not kept Riveen from insisting that Draven and Titus stay with him. For someone who usually came off as flighty, Riveen had a steel spine and a rigid determination that was…surprising.

As if thinking of him had conjured him, Riveen stepped out of the hall and grinned as he nodded at Titus.

Whatever that meant, Titus had no idea, but he smiled back.

Riveen raised both eyebrows then whispered, "Cousins are here. Sleeping beauty is going to get a loud surprise if you don't wake him up first."

"Cousins?" Titus was already gently shaking Draven's shoulder despite how much he wished Draven could sleep. He had no doubt Riveen wasn't exaggerating. Titus heard footsteps and voices from outside. "Hey, honey, Riveen said your cousins are here."

Draven sat up so fast that he almost clipped Titus' chin. "Cousins?" He yawned, stretched, and his back popped a few times. "Cousins?" he repeated, blinking then scowling. "Rive, what did you do?"

Riveen rolled his eyes. "You know what I did. Called in the reinforcements. Well. Called some of them in from spy duty. The paternal side are still out hunting for Joel. Mom's side are here to help us with…anyone else."

Titus stood and held a hand out to Draven. Draven took it and got up as well.

He cupped Titus' cheek. "Sorry, but you're about to get bombarded with my crazy cousins."

Titus was pretty sure Draven was fond of those cousins, too, judging by the sweet curve to his smile.

Then Titus was gawping at the number of people entering the room. There had to be close to two dozen. "Holy crap," he whispered. He'd never had a large extended family before and was a little intimidated. A lot of the men and women resembled Draven and Riveen to some degree, though none too much.

And *all* of those cousins were looking at Titus, grinning or smirking, one or two leering comically.

Titus gulped and raised one hand in a weak wave. "Um. Hi?"

Those two words split open the conversation and everyone began talking almost at once.

"Tried to warn you," Draven said before he nodded to Riveen.

Riveen stuck his fingers in his mouth and let loose an eardrum-splitting whistle.

"This is Titus Eisenhower, my boyfriend," Draven said when everyone went silent and half of them had flipped off Riveen. "And in case you haven't been told, he knows about us."

A short dark-haired man stepped forward and canted a hip. "Oh yeah? So he knows we're all *amazing* in bed?"

Draven groaned and turned to Titus. "Sorry. They're emotionally stuck at a mid-teenager level of development."

"Beg your pardon, cuz," a blonde woman said. "I'm at *least* emotionally eighteen."

"Don't get started," Draven pleaded with his cousins.

Riveen nodded. "Yeah. He just lost his home. Maybe now isn't the time to be smartasses."

"He started it," someone muttered.

Riveen glared in the direction the voice had come from. "And *I'm* ending it. We need help, not harassment."

That seemed to get through to everyone, and soon most of the cousins were sitting on the floor or furniture, with a few remaining standing.

"Tell us what's happened." The man who'd made the comment about being good — no, *amazing* — in bed, nodded at Titus. "I'm Dariel, by the way."

"Nice to meet you," Titus responded.

"We'll do introductions later," Riveen cut in when another person started to introduce themselves. "First, we need to be informed and come up with a plan to keep *all* of us safe, because if Andres has found a way to come back—"

"What?" A cacophony of questions and denials erupted.

Riveen held his fingers up and everyone stopped before he punished their eardrums again. "Anyone know if reincarnation is possible, or if there're other supernatural beings capable of being ripped to pieces by sharks then, you know, not dying?"

"Aunt Jusis might know," Dariel replied, frowning. "I don't know if she's back from St. Croix yet."

"She's supposed to be. Let me try to get a hold of her."

Titus didn't even try to figure out who said that.

"We saw him die," Dariel continued. "He never smelled like a shifter, and anyway, what shifter could recover from that?"

"A starfish shifter?"

Dariel glared at the speaker. "Get serious. He wasn't a shifter, and if he's alive, or back, or whatever, then he was—is—something else. Are y'all sure it was Andres? Explain that."

As Titus listened, adding in his memory of the encounter when he needed to, he began to feel less intimidated and more comfortable. Despite the trauma of the past twenty-four hours, a small ember of optimism was glowing in him.

There were so many people eager to help them, supporting them. It restored a piece of Titus' lost faith in some of humanity he hadn't even realized was missing.

But he'd seen things as a teacher that had left his heart and hopes bruised, just as he'd lost a lot of innocence at the hands of Joel.

Now, there was a small army gathered around, bantering and bouncing ideas off each other, and they all treated him like they did the rest of their family.

Despite all the bad things that had happened, Draven was smiling beside him, his eyes lit up with joy as he spoke to Dariel.

Then Draven looked at him, and that joy turned into something much stronger and enduring.

Maybe it was crazy to find peace in a time and situation such as the one they were in now, but Titus did. He saw the future in Draven's eyes, and Titus would fight for that, even if it meant taking on a supernatural being that might somehow be immortal, or close to it.

And even if it meant taking on Joel face to face.

Draven was worth it, and Titus was, too.

Chapter Thirty-Three

As he waited for Titus to get out of the bathroom, Draven thought over the past few hours they'd spent with some of his cousins. Aunt Jusis had promised to do some research—she apparently had books, *actual* books, written centuries ago that contained supernatural secrets.

Draven had always thought Aunt Jusis was a little…spooky. As a kid, he'd had the feeling she could see right into his brain and know what he was thinking. Now, he suspected she was simply very knowledge-able and world-wise. He wanted to get to know her better, and Titus had said the same thing.

Waiting for information, or another attack, made Draven twitchy as hell. He was still reeling from the loss of his home, but every time he got angry or upset, he reminded himself that the house was just a thing. The people he loved were safe, unharmed, and that was what was important. The house could be rebuilt.

And maybe some supernatural beings could be rebuilt, too.

Before he could be any more freaked out by that thought, the bathroom door swung open. Titus—as handsome as moonlight on the ocean, and just as calming to Draven's soul—stood in the doorway. Draven's thoughts scattered then quickly coalesced into the realization that he had much more urgent things to focus on just then. Titus, just by being himself, eased the pain of loss and the anxiety—and anger—that Draven had been struggling with.

"Your family is"—Titus laughed as he walked over to the bed—"huge."

"Uh-huh." Draven barely heard what Titus said. His pulse was a rushing sound in his head as he stared at Titus, who was wearing nothing but a towel wrapped around his hips.

Titus had one thumb tucked under the center front of the towel, like he'd been running his hand down his belly when someone wrapped him up.

As soon as he was within reach, Draven reached for him. Titus' skin was warm and damp from water droplets he'd missed while drying off.

Draven settled his hands on Titus' hips and raked his gaze over Titus' lean form, up to his penetrating eyes…then back to his frown.

Draven rubbed his thumbs over Titus' hip bones.

"We can't…" Titus began, his cheeks blooming with color.

"We totally can," Draven countered before leaning forward and scraping his cheek over Titus' terrycloth-covered groin. "We *so* can."

Titus slid one palm to the back of Draven's neck. He didn't push Draven away, but held him in place. "We shouldn't. We're guests and—"

Draven mouthed the tip of Titus' cock through the towel. "We should," he rumbled against it. He parted the towel and it fell to the floor…and Draven licked the length of Titus' shaft.

Titus shivered and pulled Draven closer. "Okay, we can do *something*, but we have to be quiet."

Draven gave him a sideways look. "I'm not the one going on."

Titus bumped his hips forward. "You could lie down and let me suck you, too."

As if he needed to suggest that twice! Draven scooted back and stretched out on the bed. Titus joined him, not flipping head to toes like Draven expected, but lying chest-to-chest with him before kissing Draven with a quiet ferocity that was all the more intense for it.

Draven wrapped his arms around Titus and rolled him on top. He parted his legs so Titus could settle between them with ease. Their cocks were aligned almost perfectly. Draven bent his legs at the knee and thrust up while he ran his hands down Titus' back to his plump ass. He grabbed both cheeks and began to knead in time to his thrusts, matching those with every flick of his tongue.

Titus framed Draven's face between his palms and nipped at Draven's tongue.

Draven bucked and held on to Titus harder, pushing and pulling his cheeks apart. He wanted to fuck Titus, but what they were doing felt too amazing to stop.

No, he didn't want to fuck Titus. He wanted to be close to him, closer than lovers could be.

And he was, because the love he felt for Titus was equal to the love Titus had for him. It formed an ever-flowing circle between them, growing stronger with every passing day.

That love made every touch *more*. No sex in Draven's past could even come close to what he felt with Titus.

Titus nibbled on his tongue and Draven dipped his fingers into Titus' crease. He found the tight little hole nestled there and teased his fingertips over it as Titus rutted faster.

Draven's cock ached with the need for friction, but he wasn't letting go of Titus' ass. The sounds slipping from Titus' mouth into his sent Draven's need ratcheting higher. He wound his legs around Titus', hooked his ankles over Titus' calves and began thrusting up with more force.

Titus turned his head aside and gasped. He shoved himself up onto his hands and used the change in position to rut harder.

Draven had to let go of his ass and instead fisted Titus' dick and his own.

Pleasure curled, hot and bright, in his groin. Draven wanted to keep watching Titus, but as his climax built, his eyelids kept sliding closed.

Titus grunted and a drop of sweat dripped from him onto Draven's cheek.

Draven tightened his grip on their cocks and thumbed the head of Titus'.

A short moan escaped Titus before the sound was cut off. Titus thrust again, shoving his cock desperately in Draven's hold. Draven twisted his hand around the glans, and Titus jerked all over as cum jetted over Draven's skin and splattered against his stomach.

Before Draven could do more than open his eyes, Titus was sliding down, tugging Draven's hand off his own shaft, then swallowing half of Draven's length in one quick move.

Draven didn't make it past a second thrust. He just managed to bury one hand in Titus' hair before he came, his orgasm turning Draven inside out with waves of pleasure.

When he stopped shaking and could breathe somewhat normally, Draven opened his eyes and turned to see Titus propped up beside him and scowling as he touched his head.

Draven frowned then heated with embarrassment. "Oh shit! I didn't even notice —"

Titus' scowl morphed into a grin. "Yeah. Do you know how hard dried cum is to get out of hair?"

"Yeah, I do. Lost more than a few pubes that way, too." Draven sat up. "Damn. Guess this means we need to shower. Together. That way I can make sure your hair gets de-spunked."

Titus snorted and wiped a spot of jizz over Draven's left nipple. He winked at Draven, then licked the mess up.

Heat spiraled out from Draven's nipple, zinging straight down to his cock, which wasn't up to round two yet.

"Shower," He rasped, because a naked, slippery Titus would certainly make Draven's cock perk back up.

But before they made it to the bathroom, Draven's phone rang.

Titus was closer to it. He plucked Draven's cell phone off the dresser. Seeing Deputy Martinez's name for the caller ID sent adrenalin rushing through his veins. He answered the phone with a clipped, "Hello," which was the best he could do when he knew bad news was coming. There'd be no other reason for Martinez to call.

"This is Deputy Martinez. Is this—?"

"Titus."

"Titus," Deputy Martinez repeated.

Draven cupped Titus' cheek. "It's going to be okay," he whispered.

Titus hoped Draven was right.

"I'm going to put you on speaker so Draven can hear this," Titus said.

"I wanted to let you know that I don't think Joel started the fire at Mr. Costille's residence. Joel was arrested last night in Michigan for assaulting another man, someone he'd apparently hooked up with. From what the detective I spoke with said, Joel's been in Michigan for several days."

"How many days?" Draven asked. "Was he ever in Texas?"

"Yes, from what I've been able to trace, he was, but..." Deputy Martinez sighed. "I'm trying to get flight records, but Detective Adams—in Michigan— said he thinks Joel's parents are covering his tracks. They aren't cooperating and have a lawyer snarling at Detective Adams any time he tries to gather evidence."

"Their boy can do no wrong," Titus mumbled, backing toward the bed.

"They're not doing him any favors," Martinez said. "There's something else. It might upset you more."

"Shit." Titus was glad Draven was there, guiding him down to sit on the bed.

"What is it?" Draven asked, taking a seat beside him.

Martinez sighed. "The guy he assaulted, he looks similar to you, Titus. Detective Adams emailed me a photo of him. There's a clear resemblance. Adams said the victim told him Joel called him by your name."

Titus felt ill. He pressed a hand against his queasy stomach. "But he isn't here. In Texas. He wasn't here yesterday."

"Not for the past few days," Martinez said. "I'm working on finding out just how long he's been out of the state, but I just learned that he was in Michigan about an hour ago. I've been on the phone and emailing back and forth with Detective Adams. He also thinks Joel's parents will bail him out."

"They will if they can." Titus knew that much. "He's violating his parole, though, isn't he?"

"Yeah, but if the victim backs out..." Martinez trailed off.

Titus rubbed his eyes, hoping to push back tears he didn't want to shed. "That could happen. Joel's parents offered me money not to prosecute him."

"Did you turn them in to the police for that?" Martinez asked.

"No. I didn't have any proof, and they had their lawyer in the room when they did it. My word would have been useless against the three of them," Titus said. "And in the end, I don't think it would have made a difference. A lot of people saw Joel. His parents wanted me to say it was a one-time thing, and I wouldn't."

"He didn't get a long enough sentence." Draven glared at the phone like it had personally failed in that task.

"We do the best we can, then the sentencing is out of our hands," Martinez replied. "I just wanted to let y'all know about this since it means someone else had to start the fire. Unless he paid someone to do it."

"I wouldn't put it past him," Titus admitted. "And getting arrested...that seems an extreme way to prove he wasn't here, but Joel isn't reasonable."

"Is there anyone else who'd have set the fire?" Martinez cursed. "Shit. I guess that's not information I need, unless it ties in to what happened here. I'm still waiting on prints—if it turns out that Joel's aren't among them, that doesn't mean he didn't do it. He could have worn gloves. But is there a chance it could have been someone else?"

Titus and Draven exchanged glances. "No one I can think of," Titus answered, because even if Andres *was* magically—supernaturally—alive, would he have known about Titus then? And how would Titus explain Andres to Deputy Martinez? He couldn't.

"I don't believe in coincidences," Martinez was saying. "It could be two different people harassing y'all, or it could be one person. Could be someone we haven't looked into or that you don't even know, Titus. People can be hateful and justify it to themselves in ways no rational being ever would."

Titus agreed and after a few more minutes, Deputy Martinez ended the call. Titus set the phone on the nightstand and slumped over, his elbows on his knees and his head in his hands. "I don't understand. I thought Joel was here."

Draven slid a hand up and down his back. "We don't know that he didn't have a hand in what happened."

"We don't know..." Titus sat up and leaned against Draven. "We don't know anything, yet I'm sure Joel broke into and vandalized my house. I'd been terrified I led him here, but now, knowing it wasn't him...I'm more terrified. If it wasn't him—but he could have hired someone, but the guy, the one who looked like Andres, would he do that? Why would he? How? What's—?"

Titus took a deep breath and exhaled slowly, then he did it again.

If he didn't stop, he was going to think himself into a panic attack.

Draven pulled him close and held him, and, though no words were spoken, listening to Draven's heartbeat calmed Titus down.

Chapter Thirty-Four

Draven's nape itched with that feeling he got when he was being watched. He and Titus *were* being watched—Draven's cousins were discreetly following them on land, and some were in the ocean, close to the shore. Riveen had mentioned some friends of the family—friends who were aviary shifters—keeping an eye on them from the air and trees, or wherever the birds might be.

"Lots of birds there," Titus whispered, nodding toward the large garbage bin by the ruins of Draven's house. Crows and seagulls were plentiful, as well as a couple of tricolor herons and great egrets.

Draven couldn't tell right off the bat which ones were just birds. He'd have to be closer to them to discern that, and now wasn't the time.

"The cleanup crew is going to be here in a few minutes," Riveen said as he jogged over to join them.

There'd been a long discussion about whether Riveen should be with Draven and Titus, but the consensus was that, had there been any kind of emergency, Riveen would have been at his brother's side. For him to be elsewhere would have been suspicious.

"How many people did we hire?" Draven asked as he took Titus' hand in his.

Riveen stopped a couple of feet away and swiped at his forehead. "The company I called is sending a group of ten people, a backhoe and some other equipment. I don't remember what-all, but hopefully with them and us working on it, we'll get most of this cleaned up in the next few days."

"I hate that you lost your home." Titus moved closer until they were standing shoulder to shoulder.

Draven knew Titus meant it, even though they'd outlined a rough plan for conversational topics in case they were overheard by the enemy—whomever that was. "Thank you, sweetheart. Everything is gone, but together, we'll rebuild, and we'll make a home that you and I both design. It'll be our home." And it would. Draven wanted that, wanted Titus, forever.

After searching his eyes for a moment, Titus smiled. "I want a cat. Two cats."

"That wasn't—" Draven pressed his lips together.

Riveen snickered. "Good job, Titus. You should have at least two cats, and a couple of dogs. Oh, hedgehogs are—"

"Riveen," Draven grumbled.

"What?" Riveen tried for an innocent look but failed. "Two cats for each of you. Have you seen those Savannah cats? They're huge! That's what you need, Drave, a man's cat. Big. Tough. Half-feral. No one will doubt your masculinity when you're walking it out in public."

"What the hell are you talking about?" Draven asked. "No one walks a cat!"

Riveen shook his head. "Damn. You're gonna be a shitty cat owner. People walk their cats. Look it up online."

"Relating the size and breed of a cat to someone's masculinity is just not right," Titus said. "And I think Draven would like a ragdoll or two."

"A what? Why would I want *any* kind of doll?" Draven wondered if someone had spiked Titus' coffee.

"Ragdoll is a breed of cat," Titus explained. "You'd love them. Some people *do* walk their cats. I had a neighbor down the block from my house, he used to walk his goat on Wednesdays and Fridays, and his chicken Mondays and Tuesdays. I have pictures on my laptop I can show you sometime."

Draven was trying to figure out what to say to that offer when he saw a van pull into his driveway. "I think the cleaning crew is here."

"Look at every one of them," Riveen muttered. "You too, Titus. See if any of them give you the creeps or looks like you know who."

"That's the plan." Draven headed for the group getting out of the van.

Titus tugged his hand free.

Draven looked at him.

"We'll be there in a minute." Titus tipped his chin toward the van.

"Y'all are plotting to get cats, aren't you?" Draven asked.

Titus grinned. "Maybe."

In truth, they were giving him a chance to check the people out first. If Andres — or his doppelganger — were there, and he saw Draven alone-ish, perhaps he'd give himself away.

"Hi," he called out as he neared the cleanup crew. "I'm Draven. Who's Zach?"

"Me." A tall, older man with grey hair stepped forward and held out his hand. "Zach Morris. I'm sorry for your loss of property."

"Thank you." Draven shook Zach's hand. "I'm just glad no one was hurt. "

Zach nodded. "Yeah, things can be replaced, unlike people, and even pets. You've got the right attitude." He turned and gestured to his crew. "We'll work our asses off to make this as easy for you as possible."

"Y'all been at this a long time?" Draven asked, hoping Zach would mention any newcomers.

"Over a decade now. Got a great group working for me, and I know they'll do right by you." Zach pointed at a huge truck hauling a backhoe on a trailer. "That's gonna help a lot right there, and there's another two bins on the way. If we don't need 'em, that's okay. You're only charged for what we have to use."

"Sounds good." Draven didn't get a weird feeling from Zach or anyone nearby. He wasn't sure that meant anything. "I have my brother and boyfriend here, and some of my family will arrive in a bit to help if we need them."

Zach hadn't so much as batted an eye at the boyfriend comment. "I'll tell ya, it's best to keep people away while we work. You, your guy and your brother, that's fine, and you can have your family here, I'm not telling you you can't, but we'll have to keep an eye on them and make sure they don't get in the way or endanger themselves."

"So they'd be a distraction," Draven said. "Hmm. Well, if they show up with food and drinks, we'll keep them away from the working area."

Zach nodded. "That'll do."

Titus and Riveen walked over, and Draven introduced them to Zach, then the work began.

Draven kept close to Titus, and they tried to check out every person there. None of them were Andres, and after an hour, Draven began to think Zach and his crew were just regular people.

Working on cleaning up the debris, then clearing it out, was hard work. Riveen, Titus and Draven didn't slack off. Though Zach wanted them to stay away from the remains of the structure itself, there was still plenty of hauling and lifting to do.

When they broke for lunch, catered by Draven's family, Draven was ready for a break. He had soot in places no one ever should have it. Titus and Riveen were grungy, too.

"I swear I'll never not smell this." Titus held up a burned piece of wood, then tossed it aside.

"Same," Riveen mumbled. "My back is starting to hurt like a motherfucker."

"You can sit back and watch," Draven said.

Riveen shook his head. "Nope. Things seem calm here. Everyone is nice."

Translation — no weird vibes from anyone.

"Yeah," Draven agreed.

Titus nodded. "Very professional and friendly folks. I'm going to wash my hands then use the portable toilet. Well, use that then wash my hands. Or wash them both times — whatever. I've got to hit the head."

"We'll be here." Draven watched Titus jog over to the water hose and wash his hands, then enter the blue portable.

"He's only twenty feet away," Riveen pointed out.

"Doesn't matter. Been closer to bad people and things," Draven replied. He took a bite of the sub sandwich he'd gotten off the food table that had been set up.

"Yeah, that's true."

And even though Draven hadn't looked away for more than thirty seconds—forty, tops, as he'd taken a bite and a drink—when Titus didn't come out of the portable in three minutes, he began to worry.

"He's probably doing, you know," Riveen said, looking at the toilet. "You've been watching."

"Except for when I grabbed my sandwich and picked up my drink." Draven set the can down. He wiped his hands on his shorts.

"Seconds." Riveen set his food down as well. "Just seconds. He's in there."

Draven stood, and Riveen was right behind him, striding to the porta potty. Draven knew he was probably being paranoid—until he saw the door was open an inch or so.

"Titus," he rasped as he reached the door and pulled it open— and found it empty.

"Titus!" Draven shouted as he ran past the portable. There was no use in trying not to panic—fear clawed at Draven from the inside out. "Titus!"

"Draven! Draven!" Riveen grabbed his arm. "He can't be far. Maybe he just walked—"

"No!" Draven tried to shake Riveen off but couldn't. "I *feel* it, Rive. I *feel* that he's gone!"

Riveen paled. "G-gone?"

Draven snarled. "Not *that* kind of gone!" Draven was certain he'd know, but the idea of a world without Titus in it bruised his heart and soul. "He's been taken!"

"Who'd take him?"

Draven spun around and almost slammed into Zach. "What?"

Zach frowned. "You're yellin' for your boyfriend and said he'd been taken. Who'd take him? I can call the cops—"

"No," Draven snapped. "No cops."

"But if he's been kidnapped or...or whatever, then we need—"

"No," Draven reiterated, cutting off Zach's argument. "No cops, I mean it. This is...not that kind of thing."

Zach didn't look cowed. "Um, what kind of thing is it, then?" He folded his thick arms over his chest.

Riveen squeezed Draven's arm just as Draven opened his mouth to put Zach on blast.

"This is a game we play with some friends of ours, fake abductions," Riveen said. His smile looked strained, but hopefully Zach wouldn't notice. "It's like a treasure hunt. We have to find clues and track them down, then we get Titus back and formulate our revenge."

"That's messed up," Zach muttered, staring at Draven.

Dariel was approaching behind Zach. "It is, but that's how we roll. We're a group of weirdos."

Zach turned to look at him. "I guess, whatever floats your boat."

"Yeah, so we need to get on with our scavenger hunt. I'm sure y'all can do your job without us taggin' along," Dariel said.

"Of course we can." Zach glanced back at Draven and Riveen.

Draven wanted to punch Zach for causing a delay. Instead, he nodded. As far as he was concerned, he was done answering questions.

"The family's already spread out and looking," Dariel whispered when Zach headed back to his lunch. "As soon as you realized he was gone. Come on." He took off, and Draven was right beside him, with Riveen there as well.

And probably all the rest of the cousins that'd been hanging around the cleanup site.

Draven looked as he ran, searching for any trace of Titus — or Andres. He saw birds flying overhead, heard them calling out and recognized their voices.

His family was there, had been there and yet, Titus was gone.

"What kind of fuckery are we fighting against?" he mumbled.

Dariel pointed to the house at the end of the block. "Stop there, around the corner."

Draven didn't want to stop. He wanted to find Titus and not rest until he held him in his arms.

"Stop," Dariel growled. "We need to formulate a plan. Otherwise, we're running around like a bunch of chickens with their heads cut off."

Several birds squawked at that.

Draven stopped around the corner. "I have to find him. I *have* to find him, *now!*"

"Right," Riveen agreed, grabbing him and giving him a shake. "So let's figure out how best to do that."

"How?" Draven laughed but there was nothing other than fear in the sound. "We don't even know who has him for sure. If it's Andres, we don't fucking know *what* Andres is!"

Birds settled around them.

"He has to be magic. He couldn't have been only a human being. Andres had to have been more, and maybe...maybe he became something stronger upon his death," Riveen said.

"Like a goddamn evil phoenix," Dariel added. "No one has heard from Aunt Jusis. Damn it, what would she do?"

"I don't care what she'd do—we have to find Titus!" Draven was ready to punch someone. He'd never felt so helpless before, and his anger was only held in check by his fear for Titus.

"Yes, we do. It's—" Dariel hissed when one of the birds began to shift. "Not in public!" He moved to shield her from anyone who might have been watching. Riveen helped him.

"We fight magic with magic."

Draven recognized the voice of his cousin Ninfa.

"I am sorry I only just arrived to help. I came as quickly as I could, and that's enough on that. You must remember, we are supernatural beings, too," she said.

"That's not helping us find Titus," Draven bit out.

Ninfa peered over Dariel's shoulder. "We are looking with the wrong part of ourselves. We are shifters. We were created with a drop of blood from Alquinones—have you forgotten?"

Draven had heard the tale a dozen times. "That's just a—"

"Not *just* anything," Ninfa interrupted. "It's not a fable. It's our past, our creation. It's real, and we carry the blood of the animal god in our veins."

"So what does that do to help us?" Draven wasn't going to argue. If there was any chance Ninfa was right, that she could do something to help find Titus, then Draven would listen.

"Magic all comes from the same place, from the first moment of time, when the great goddess gave birth and particles collided and energy spiraled out in great and lesser amounts," Ninfa explained. "The greater energy became our demigods, and the lesser, humans and animals, all life as we know it. Alquinones wanted his own people, and we are the result of the compromise he struck with the great goddess. You have heard this before."

Draven ground his teeth. He'd heard it before, and time was being wasted on the story now, when action was what was needed.

"We can find him," Ninfa said. "Through our blood. Through your blood, Draven, because it is your mate who is missing. Come here and someone give me a knife."

Chapter Thirty-Five

Ninfa had to be Aunt Jusis' protégé. She had the aura of power, of magic, all around her.

She chanted and the air seemed to waver and spread out in a circle. "So we will not be seen," she explained after the ripples had surrounded the family. "Marybelle, a feather, please."

A heron waddled over and fluffed out her feathers. She squawked when Ninfa plucked a tail feather free.

"You'll grow it back quickly." Ninfa held the feather up in the palm of her left hand. With her right, she traced the quill, then blew on the feather. It should have become airborne, but it didn't—immediately. After she raised her right hand and wiggled her fingers, the feather floated up and spun around several times.

"Follow it," Ninfa said before shifting again.

The rippled air around them vanished and the feather dipped and spun as if being carried on a breeze.

The cousins in bird form ascended and flapped their wings lazily. Draven, Riveen and Dariel, along with a few other cousins, watched the feather and began following it when it moved.

It was slow going, and sometimes the feather hesitated, turning this way and that before resuming its path.

Draven wanted it to move faster, but he wasn't stupid enough to bitch about speed. Magic was his best hope of finding Titus, and snarling at a magical feather wasn't going to help.

They were led around the center of town, and maybe they looked like a pack of tourists strolling along, not that it mattered. The feather didn't seem to be noticed by anyone they passed, and no one would think anything of a flock of birds flying overhead.

Once they'd cleared the small downtown area, the feather turned toward the beach. Draven's heart raced as he considered what that could mean. Titus was human—he wouldn't survive submersion. Would Andres—whoever, whatever he was—care about that? What was Andres' goal, anyway?

Draven wished he knew.

Riveen touched his arm as if to reassure him everything would be okay, but Draven wasn't sure he could trust that.

"I can't lose him," he rasped as they cut a corner. The dunes rose up in front of them. "I can't."

"You won't," Riveen assured him.

Draven opened his mouth to say what, he didn't know, when the sky went as dark as night and a cold wind slapped against him. "What the fuck?"

The feather shot up in the air and a bolt of lightning struck it, singeing it into a blackened pile of ash that scattered on the breeze.

"Shit," Draven muttered as his cousins and Riveen all began talking at once.

Ninfa shifted again, as did the rest of the cousins. They gathered close and Ninfa held out one hand. "Silence. Everyone is talking, and nothing is being said."

No one cracked a joke or even exhaled loudly.

Ninfa nodded, her gaze locked with Draven's. "His magic is stronger than mine, but it is not stronger than *ours*. He has brought us into his reality." She gestured around them.

The beach was familiar in some ways, but foreign in others. The dunes looked ominous, as if they'd rise on legs of thorns and pull down anyone who stepped on them — or got too close. Creatures skittered across the sand, but they weren't the crabs Draven was used to seeing. They were dingy red, with dozens of glowing white eyes and pinchers that looked like blades.

Something that looked like seaweed jetted out strands that caught up one of the creatures, and it shrieked before disappearing into the mass of vegetation.

"Maybe we shouldn't be standing around," Dariel said nervously.

"They can't harm us." Ninfa didn't sound as certain as Draven would have liked.

Something roared out in the murky water, making everyone wrench their head around to look.

"Fuck me," Riveen muttered.

Draven felt dizzy as he stared at the — he could only define it as a sea monster, a bastardization of animals Mother Nature had created, twisted and blended into a living nightmare.

"Is…is that real?" someone asked.

Ninfa began to chant.

Another living nightmare arose from the water. It had teeth like a great white, and dozens of white eyes like the things on the beach.

Lightning shot across the sky and struck the beach where the waves were lingering at the shore. The wind whipped harder, lashing out, but no thunder sounded from above.

The ground quaked under his feet, and Draven tore his gaze from the beasts to the sand under his feet. It shifted and he half-expected to be swallowed up, but no gaping holes appeared.

Draven hated the fear that pummeled his chest. Anger washed it away, and he raised his head, glaring at the monsters as he shouted, "What the hells do you want from me?"

He wasn't certain if anyone heard the laughter besides him. "Andres! Show yourself, you fucking coward!" Draven took a step toward the water.

The first beast roared and lunged at him. It wasn't close enough to reach him—he hoped—but not running away was difficult. Draven's instincts screamed at him that he was in danger. He ignored them and took another step, then a third. "Andres!"

Riveen moved to stand beside him. "This is crazy. This is crazy. How—?"

The water churned, and the two beasts scurried back into its depths.

"Uh oh. If something is coming that scared those two off…" Riveen gripped Draven's arm. "I can't—"

He gasped, as did Draven, when a wave rose, towering so high it looked like it blended into the dark sky above.

Draven saw things in that wave — hate, and anger, images of Andres, and his death.

And his brother, Riveen, watching over the sharks as Andres was torn to pieces, as his blood turned the ocean water red around him.

"Rive —" Draven began, fear burning cold in his gut. He got no further before the wave lashed out. Draven turned and grabbed at Riveen, whose eyes were wide and nearly bulging, and his mouth open as he tried to speak.

The wave snatched him out of Draven's grasp. "Riveen!" Draven slapped at air as his brother was taken into the ocean.

"No!" Draven shouted, his throat burning as fear tore through him. "*No!*" He ran, the wind battering him back a step despite his attempt to move forward. "Andres! You fucking bastard, fight me!"

He couldn't see Riveen in the wave, didn't know if he was alive or dead, hurting or scared— "Andres!"

"He's not going to give in that easy," Dariel bellowed. "He wants to hurt you!"

"Argh!" Draven pushed against the wind. Grains of sand pummeled him, stinging where they cut his face, hands and legs.

Ninfa raised her hands, and Draven caught a glimpse of her eyes glowing black, the color seeming to leach into the air around her. The words she spoke were ones he didn't recognize, a language he didn't know. Bolts of blue and black shot from her fingertips, hitting the wave and setting off sparks of gold and green as a great wailing sound poured from the wave.

It split in two, and Riveen fell into the churning ocean.

Draven and Dariel surged forward when the wind ebbed for a moment.

The water was cold, not like the Gulf of Mexico had ever been. Chills raced over Draven as he waded in. Slimy tendrils of something wrapped around his ankles. Thorns or teeth or claws hooked into his skin.

Draven jerked one foot free, then the other, but every step he took only led to another attack by whatever was under the water.

Dariel screamed. "No!"

Draven and several cousins grabbed at Dariel as he began to sink.

On the beach behind him, a great light shone, bright yet dark. Its rays hit the sky, and a great *BOOM* ripped through the other chaotic sounds. Dozens of explosions occurred overhead. Red, white and yellow balls shot out and burst, the colors raining down on the ocean like someone had upturned a glitter container.

Someone managed to pull Dariel up before he sank past his chest. Draven gasped at the wounds on his cousin. There had to be a hundred cuts, gashes—bites, he didn't know what they were, but Dariel was bleeding, and his eyes were open yet unfocused. For one horrible second, he thought Dariel was dead, then Dariel shrieked at being hoisted up onto another cousin's shoulder.

Draven's ankles were burning. Whatever had been attacking him was still there. He saw Riveen's body bob on a wave and his heart plummeted. "*Riveen!*"

Then Riveen was gone as the wave pulled him under.

Beside Draven, his cousin Elric screamed and the panicked attempt to save him from being sucked under began.

"Go," Valeria shouted at him. "Go get Riveen!"

Draven jerked one foot loose, then the tendrils dragged across his other ankle, tearing at it, before suddenly disappearing. Draven took a deep breath, then dove into the coming wave, praying to whatever deities existed to save Titus, Riveen and their cousins.

As soon as Draven went under, he shifted. He could maneuver through the rough water easier as a manta ray. He saw the spiked tendrils that had harmed him, saw glowing white eyes and fangs, monsters he couldn't comprehend or ever forget.

But they didn't touch him, despite their attempts to do so. A thin layer of black had spread out under him, Ninfa's magic shielding him as he swam.

Tears burned his eyes when he spotted Riveen. Shifted as well, Riveen was alive, but he wasn't able to swim with both wings, and a gash ran along the side he couldn't use.

He's alive. He's alive, and he'll recover –

Draven's thoughts were shattered as an arm shot past him.

Just an arm.

It took a moment for his brain to process what that meant.

A cloud of blood flowed beside him.

No! *No!* He didn't know who it was, but his cousins were the only human-like beings around...besides Titus. *Not him. Not anyone!*

Draven couldn't understand this nightmare, couldn't grasp how violent and deadly it was, how much pain and suffering – and loss – would come of it.

He saw Riveen recoil from the arm and rushed toward him.

More blood. Draven gagged. Was it real, or was it a trick? The blood was so thick around him and Riveen, it was difficult to see.

He heard a splash and tried to touch Riveen. Then the water surged around them, and everything tilted.

Riveen was slammed against him. Draven couldn't have moved away — he and Riveen had been caught in a net. They both thrashed, but to no avail. The net didn't ascend, but rather flew deeper into the ocean.

Draven stilled as monstrous things flitted past — or he and Riveen shot past *them. What kind of hell is this? What kind of magic? This is a whole different realm, or different reality. The cold temperature alone should kill me and Riveen —*

Visions appeared in the swirling waves. Draven tried to cry out as he saw a hook strike Ninfa, saw other cousins fighting off a great, many-clawed beast. It used one pincher to rip off a leg. Draven's cousin screamed as blood spurted everywhere.

No! It can't be real. It can't be! Riveen shivered beside him. Draven tried to comfort him, but there was no comfort to be had when nightmares play out all around them.

He saw the slaughter of every one of his cousins — those who had been with him on the beach, and those searching and trying to find out anything they could to help. It had to be unreal, at least part of it did, because no being could be so powerful.

Draven shifted, and the water didn't fill his lungs when he inhaled. "It's not real," he said. "Riveen, it isn't real."

Riveen shifted and cringed. "Fuck it isn't. This is real." He pressed a hand to his left arm, the biceps of which had sustained a deep cut. "This is real, but — "

"Not all of it." Draven grabbed the netting and pulled. It didn't rip as he'd hoped it would.

"That thing that had me was real," Riveen muttered. "I hope…"

"Me too." Draven knew what Riveen hoped — they didn't want to lose their cousins. *That arm that I saw, the battle on the beach — none of that's real.*

Riveen pressed his hand over his mouth, then turned away and heaved.

Draven wrapped his arms around his brother. "Don't look. Don't watch. He's fucking with our heads."

Riveen turned toward him and curled against Draven. "What if it's all real?"

Draven didn't have an answer. He held Riveen and closed his eyes as the net sped through the water.

Chapter Thirty-Six

Cold. Titus shivered. His head ached, and the cold seemed to seep all the way to his core. He tried to open his eyes, and maybe he succeeded, or maybe he was still unconsciousness—he couldn't tell. There was nothing but the darkness, not even a speck of light. With his head pounding, he couldn't think, couldn't focus. All he knew was confusion, darkness, and the cold.

Suddenly, a light so bright that it hurt his eyes hit Titus. He cringed and tried to place his hands over his eyes even though he closed them again, but he couldn't move his arms.

"Wh—?" He coughed and licked his dry lips. There wasn't enough spit in his mouth to lubricate them. Titus' throat was equally dry. It burned and, he realized a second later, most of his body felt hot and ached and he couldn't move much at all.

His last memory before waking was of being with Draven at the site of his burned-down house. There was nothing after that. His heart pounded as he tried to work his hands free. Pain shot through his wrists and shoulders. He started to open one eye, but the sound of movement nearby stopped him.

"I know you're awake. Open your eyes."

Titus shivered upon hearing that cold, toneless voice.

"Now." A sharp slap to his cheek startled Titus into doing what he'd been told to do.

Squatting before him — and blocking out most of the godawful light — was the man from the grocery store parking lot. His eyes were entirely white, with no hint of other color or pupils. "Yes, you see me, Titus. I know who you are. How could I not when Draven screams so pitifully for you?"

Titus was terrified, but he wouldn't be cowed. "You sound like the worst movie villain ever."

That comment got him another slap.

Titus' ears rang, and he tasted blood. At least it wetted his parched mouth. "Act like it, too."

He expected another slap. He didn't get one.

"What is it about you that makes him love you?"

Titus still didn't hear any emotion in the man's voice. "I'm not like you." *Andres. It's Andres.*

Andres bared his teeth, showing two rows of sharp fangs. "You are weak."

Titus slowly shook his head. Those teeth were no doubt capable of ripping out someone's throat. "No, I'm not. Compassion and kindness aren't weaknesses."

"They are not strengths," Andres countered. He cupped Titus' chin in a grip that hurt. "I knew he did not love me. I wanted to hurt him."

"He *did* love you," Titus answered, though it was hard to speak with the grip Andres had on him. He had to tilt his head back to have any jaw movement. "That's why it took decades for him to love again." He didn't think he was lying. Draven might not have loved Andres like he loved Titus, but there'd been *some* love there. "You were going to expose him and his family to humans."

Andres shrugged and tightened his fingers against Titus' chin. "And he killed me. Riveen watched as the sharks tore me apart. Do you have any idea of the agony I experienced? Physically, mentally, emotionally? Though I will admit, I did not lose the love of my life." He smiled, then flicked a four-pronged tongue over his lips. "That I found after my death, and now, I've been granted my revenge."

None of that made any sense to Titus. "You want to do what was done to you? After how that made you feel?"

Andres leaned in and instead of licking his own lips again, he licked Titus' with that creepy tongue. "You taste like fear and desperation. Wonderful."

Titus tried to turn his head aside but couldn't. Andres ran his tongue up Titus' cheek, over one eye, then down to his ear.

"Stop," Titus rasped before he could stop himself. "Don't touch me!"

Andres licked a path down his neck, then sat back, still holding Titus' chin. "Are you afraid for your virtue? That was not sexual. I know your taste and scent now. There is nowhere you can go that I cannot find you."

Titus doubted he'd be going anywhere other than a grave unless something miraculous happened.

Andres smiled and let go of his chin only to slap him again. "You are the bait, Titus. I do not care whether you live or die—yet—but Draven and Riveen, and all their family? Those are the ones I will take pleasure in killing. Draven last, of course. I want him to see the destruction of all he loves."

Then why isn't he going to kill me? Titus wanted to ask, but Andres cocked his head, listening to something Titus couldn't hear, then he stood.

"My lover arrives," Andres said.

At first Titus thought he meant Draven, because Andres was obviously a fucking mess, but then a dark shape emerged to the left—a dark, hulking shape that easily dwarfed Titus and Andres.

"Tokokuen," Andres murmured, holding out a hand to the form.

It wasn't quite man and wasn't any creature Titus had ever seen. He couldn't quite make out the shape, the edges and lines, the limbs or head. It was as if his brain couldn't comprehend what his eyes saw, and there was a revolt occurring between his neurons and the other grey matter.

But Andres was moving, gliding toward that figure. "Tokokuen, you are here. I didn't expect you."

The sound that came from the thing—from Tokokuen—caused shards of agony to splinter in Titus' head. He screamed, then darkness enveloped him again.

Chapter Thirty-Seven

It looked like they were going to be crushed against a huge stone wall. Draven wrapped his arms around Riveen and tried to shield him, hoping to save him.

A drag on the net jolted them backward, then the wall parted and blinding light spilled out from the crack.

Draven couldn't keep his eyes open. Riveen struggled in his embrace, but wounded as he was, he wasn't able to break free.

The net surged forward. Draven's stomach dipped right before he and Riveen came to a halt. Draven tried to look, but the light was too strong.

"Are we alive?" Riveen whispered, squirming.

Draven turned to the side and tried opening his eyes again. The light was horrible, but he could bear it from that position. "We are." Goosebumps pebbled his skin. Something else was there with him and Riveen.

Draven turned them away and cupped Riveen's head, pushing it to one side since Riveen would be facing the worst of the light. Draven used his body once again to shield Riveen, then Draven's breath rushed from his lungs and his knees went weak as he saw Titus, bound and unconscious not a dozen feet away. Blood trickled from his left temple, and a darkening bruise marred one side of his face. His clothing was torn and hanging in shreds, but he was alive, and Draven clung to that.

"Let me have my revenge. You promised me this." Draven heard from behind him, and he knew that voice, had once anticipated hearing it.

A chaotic sound followed, and it made Draven's head throb as if it were about to burst.

"Fuck. Fuck, ow!" Riveen's legs gave out, and Draven went with him to the floor. The net kept them off most of it, but what Draven felt beside that was slimy and cold.

"We will let the human go," Andres was saying to someone. "If I must."

Another rumbling followed, and Draven had to cradle his head with both hands. Riveen whimpered and started to shiver.

"It is not fair," Andres snapped. "Why should any of them be freed?"

The third time that foreign sound occurred, Riveen's entire body convulsed. Draven only had a moment to feel the utter depths of terror before his own nervous system went haywire. The next thing he knew, he was curled up on his side, and he ached all over. The bright light was either stronger or he was just fucked up. Draven couldn't tell which, and his head hurt too bad for him to be able to think.

The air around them shimmered, wavering like heat wafting off asphalt. Riveen whimpered, and Draven rolled over, pulled to look toward the light.

Ninfa appeared, water dripping from her hair, and at first what Draven thought was seaweed sliding through her dark tresses.

Then he blinked and his vision came into focus, and he saw the dozens of thin sea snakes—*no, eels*—writhing in her hair.

"What—?" The word was hardly even a sound. Draven coughed and tried again. "What are you?" Because she wasn't just a shifter. He felt the power flowing from her, much as he'd felt the power coming from the source of the fucking light.

Ninfa didn't answer him. She moved one hand behind her and made a gesture. Draven feared he wasn't getting her message, but warmth radiated up from his toes, spreading inside him, chasing off the pain and cold.

Riveen stretched out beside him and almost glowed. Draven saw the wound to his arm heal in a matter of seconds.

"Titus," Draven whispered, crawling onto his hands and knees. Titus' wounds were gone, and his eyes were open, his gaze on Draven.

The bindings holding Titus fell off, and Titus pushed himself up. There was a silver-blue aura surrounding him for the briefest of moments, then it was gone.

Ninfa spoke, and though Draven couldn't comprehend the words, they didn't hurt him like the other thing's sounds had.

Titus glanced toward the light and blanched. He rushed over to the net and started pulling at it. "How do I get this off?"

"The more you pull, the harder it will be for us to get free. It's tightening around the bottom." Draven pointed at the enclosed end. "There's usually—"

"Here." Riveen worked at the bottom of the net, parting the gathered material there and spreading it open.

"Hurry," Titus urged. "I don't know what's happening, but none of them are paying attention to us now."

"Not true."

Titus froze. Draven pivoted, still squatting, and felt dizzy when he found himself only inches away from Andres.

Andres' eyes were colder than anything Draven could imagine. There would be no mercy from him.

Ninfa spoke again, and a thunderous roar followed her words. Draven wanted to look, to make sure she hadn't been harmed, but he was afraid to take his focus off Andres.

Andres flicked a hand at Titus and Titus tumbled onto his butt. "Get up, and I will ignore Tokokuen's order not to harm you."

"Stay down." Draven dragged his gaze from Andres to Titus. "Please, Titus." He wouldn't be able to fight Andres half as well if he were watching out for Titus.

Andres flinched as another roar filled the cave, or room — Draven hadn't paid any attention to where they were. It didn't matter. Getting Titus to safety was the priority, and making sure Riveen and Ninfa escaped, too.

"Enough waiting. I have waited over fifty years for my revenge." Andres flicked his wrist and the net vanished.

Draven put himself between Andres and Riveen. "Leave everyone else alone. This is — "

Andres bared his teeth. "This is about you, and your brother, who delighted in my death. Do you know what it felt like, to be torn into pieces, the pain and fear, the regrets…?" He shook his head slowly. "But you will."

Draven braced himself as Andres stepped forward. The kaftan-like thing he wore flowed with his movement. Draven never even saw the move coming, didn't know he'd been hit until he shot sideways, and pain bloomed hot across his cheek.

Then Riveen yelled, and Draven scrambled up, stunned from the impact when he'd landed on the ground. The slimy surface was erratic, and he slid more than once as he tried to get to Riveen.

Riveen tackled Andres — or tried to. Andres barely moved. He grinned as he grabbed Riveen's hair and jerked his head back.

Draven bellowed just as Andres' mouth opened and a nightmarish tongue slithered out. He saw Titus moving cautiously to the right, attention locked on Andres.

Riveen slammed his fists against Andres' sides. "Fuck you!"

Draven slipped and crashed into Andres. He clutched at Andres' arm and shoulder, hoping to topple him over.

Andres thrust him away, sending Draven backward and onto his ass again.

Titus crept around to behind Andres but was still several feet away.

There was no way for Draven to tell Titus to get back without giving away his position.

Behind him, Draven heard the sound of flesh striking flesh. Whatever that bright-light-bearing creature was, Ninfa had to be fighting it.

Andres laughed and gripped Riveen by the throat. "I am not human, as you have surely figured out. I was less than the least of your demigods, a blood-diluted bastard with hardly any power. And you killed me." He shook Riveen, using his hold on Riveen's neck to lift him inches off the ground before rattling him. "I suppose some might think you did me a favor, because Tokokuen favored me and brought me to him."

Draven didn't know who the fuck Tokokuen was, but he'd guess the fucking awful light was him. "Leave Riveen alone! He was protecting me!"

Andres squeezed, and Riveen kicked, clawing at Andres' wrist and hand. "No."

Draven used every ounce of his strength to throw himself at Andres.

Andres brought his other hand around and pointed. Whatever he'd planned to do was interrupted by Titus using his linked hands like a weapon and slamming them against the side of Andres' head.

Titus yelled, and Andres' eyes went wide. Draven collided with him just as Andres let go of Riveen. Together, Draven and Andres tumbled down. Draven twisted and let Andres carry the brunt of the fall.

Andres' shout was full of fury and hatred. Draven felt it as Andres' breath gushed over his face.

Whatever Andres was, he had power and it wasn't of the human or shifter variety. Draven punched and kicked—he didn't fight fair, and didn't intend to against anyone trying to kill his loved ones.

You're not going to win! Draven would have said it, but Andres hit his throat, and breathing was suddenly not possible.

Andres bellowed, and Draven managed to suck in some air as Andres' hair was yanked hard enough to pull his body upward.

Draven saw Riveen holding two handfuls of black hair now detached from Andres' head.

Then Titus came rushing over with a short copper dagger in his hand. "Here! That snake-woman tossed it to me!"

Andres bucked, and hit Draven in the stomach. Black dots appeared in his vision and nausea welled up, threatening to make him vomit in the middle of the fight. Draven gulped and wheezed as Riveen kicked Andres' arm. Titus handed the knife to Draven, and he had just enough time to note that the blade wasn't very long before Riveen screamed.

Draven stood, doubling over though he tried not to. Riveen's left arm was lumpy, broken, he realized, and Andres was laughing as he wrapped his hands around Riveen's neck.

Draven stumbled forward, trying to hold the dagger up. He didn't see how the blade could cause a fatal blow unless he hit a major artery.

But maybe he could distract Andres long enough for Riveen and Titus to get to safety.

Although nowhere would be safe from Andres, nowhere would be out of reach.

Whatever kind of world they'd been dragged into kept screwing with Titus' head. He'd been hurt, then healed in seconds. He'd been bound, then freed without a touch. There was some kind of freakishly powerful blob of white light that Ninfa was fighting, and Andres, who'd been killed so long ago, was trying to kill Draven and Riveen—and probably Titus, but right now, Andres wasn't even looking at him.

No, Andres was killing Riveen, squeezing the life out of him as Draven tried to intervene.

The copper dagger had a blade that was maybe four inches long. Titus doubted it'd do much damage to Andres—after all, he'd already died once, and here he was again. Regardless, he had to help stop Andres. Titus wasn't eager to die. If he did so today, at least he'd go out trying to save the people he loved.

Titus roared and barreled toward Andres and Riveen. Draven was coming up behind Andres, and Titus hoped to draw Andres' focus.

Andres glanced at him but didn't release Riveen.

Riveen sagged, and Titus, afraid he was dead, yelled with all the fear and anger in him. "Andres!" All other words failed him as he leapt, or tried to, sliding wildly over a slick spot—but he flailed and slammed against Andres and Riveen. The impact jarred him through and through.

Andres tossed Riveen aside like he was a bag of trash and turned on Titus. He grabbed Titus by the neck, and Titus flushed with panic at the tightening grip cutting off his air.

He fought and though it was only seconds, it felt longer until Andres shrieked, the sound tearing through Titus' brain like an ice pick. Andres let go, and Titus fell to the ground, gasping, his vision hazed. Something splattered close to him and he recoiled as the coppery scent of blood hit his nostrils. He blinked and could make out Draven pulling the dagger from Andres' neck as Andres screamed again and slapped his hands over the wound.

Draven raised the dagger, and a bolt of white light struck it. Draven yelped, and his entire body shook, the light seeming to enter into him, making him glow.

"No! Draven!" Titus shaded his eyes as best he could even as he cried out for Draven.

Andres let loose a sound unlike anything Titus had ever heard. He dropped to his knees, more blood leaking out from under his hands.

Ninfa morphed into something not human, not bird—and not harpy, but a combination that was terrifying. Her talons were copper, as was her beak. Brown liquid oozed from a dozen wounds on her wings and torso, but she moved with a speed that was astounding as she flew into the brightest part of the light.

Titus had to close his eyes then. His brain throbbed and even with his eyes closed, there was such a bright wave of light that he feared he would be blinded.

He scrambled up onto his knees, then to his feet. He had to get to Draven, had to help him fight Andres. *I can't lose him. I can't lose Draven. I can't!*

"Titus, help me," he heard Riveen say from his left. "Help me save him!"

Titus turned and opened his eyes enough to see Riveen trying to get up, arm broken, neck bruised. He wasn't far away, only a few feet. Titus stretched out an arm to him, took a step closer.

Riveen grabbed on, and Titus hoisted him upright. There was no time to formulate a plan.

"Grab him." That was all Titus could manage as he pivoted, slid, then steadied himself just long enough to get his footing. He had to take a peek at Draven, get his position in mind, then Titus rushed toward him, hoped he was in the right spot — or close to it — and he swiped up, aiming for where he thought the dagger was.

He found it with his palm, and pain seared his hand as he sliced it open.

And many things happened at once.

The bright light dimmed to a bearable level.

Ninfa cawed, speaking words that were unintelligible to Titus.

Andres sobbed loudly.

Draven was frozen for a moment, mouth open, eyes wide, expression lax, then he crumpled before Titus could reach him.

Riveen slid to his knees beside Titus. The ground shook and Riveen called out Titus' name.

Titus turned his head just in time to see Andres coming at him.

But Andres had both hands on his neck, and Titus wasn't afraid. He kicked out, catching Andres in the stomach.

Andres grunted and whether it was an automatic response or something else, he moved his hands off his neck.

The copper dagger shot past Titus and was embedded in the center of Andres' throat a split-second later.

Andres collapsed without a sound.

The light dimmed even more, and Titus scrambled over to Draven. His eyes were closed now.

"He's alive," Riveen scraped out before Titus could even ask. "He's breathing. Andres isn't. Neither whatever he brought with him here."

"It is done," Ninfa said, squatting by Draven's head. "Andres and his demigod lover Tokokuen are no more." She touched Draven's forehead and began to chant.

Titus would have questions later, but for now, all he wanted was to hold Draven and hear his voice. The sob took him by surprise as he bent over to press his cheek to Draven's.

He felt the magic — or whatever it was — Ninfa was pouring into Draven, felt the healing strength of it.

"It is enough," she murmured. "I have no more strength, but it is enough."

Draven took a deep, shuddering breath. Titus sat up and watched him open his eyes.

"Ti—" Draven coughed, and Titus pressed a finger to Draven's lips.

"I'm here. Riveen's here, Ninfa's—" Titus blinked. She wasn't there. "Alive. Andres isn't. It's over, Draven. It's over."

Chapter Thirty-Eight

Before Draven could sit up, the dark clouds parted and the wind swirled sand all around them. Not a single grain came close to him or Titus — or Riveen, who was hunched over on the ground, cradling his arm. Bruises were forming on his neck, and a bolt of fear shot through Draven. He'd almost lost his brother, and the number of casualties to their family had yet to be discerned.

"Let me help you." Titus slipped an arm under Draven and used his other hand to pull.

Draven ached all over. He didn't even try not to whimper as he moved. "Up. All the way." He'd need to get to his feet anyway, and since he was already miserable, he figured he'd just get the worst of it over with.

Although, walking wasn't going to feel so great, either.

"I can't see past this...this..." Titus tipped his chin to part of the swirling sand. "Riveen needs our help, though."

"Yeah, I can—" Draven wasn't sure he could stand on his own. He'd try.

"Lean on me," Titus urged.

Draven did, and the first step he took nearly dropped him to his knees. The second was slightly less hellacious, and the third had barely begun when the sand parted close to Riveen, and Ninfa popped in to squat beside him.

"Shit," Draven muttered. He'd never been around Ninfa much growing up, but he'd seen her about once a year at the family get-together. He'd been clueless to the fact that she was something more than the rest of them.

Now, clothed in a black and turquoise robe, her wrists, neck, and ears covered in burnt silver jewelry studded with colorful stones, tattoos snaking down her arms, Ninfa exuded power and strength.

She helped Riveen to his feet. "I'm sorry I haven't the energy left to heal you."

Riveen winced and exhaled shakily. He tried to speak and coughed so hard Ninfa had to wrap both of her arms around him. "You saved Draven," he scraped out.

"Don't speak. You need to give your throat a rest." Ninfa closed her eyes. "Now."

Riveen looked like he was going to ask a question— much like Draven wanted to ask, Now what?

But the winds kicked up for a moment, then just as quickly as they'd started, they stopped.

And Draven's head spun.

"How—what—?" Titus swayed either in shock or under Draven's weight, or both.

Draven tried to stand up on his own.

"Home," Riveen squeaked.

Ninfa tutted. "No talking."

"Where are the others?" Draven asked as Titus led him to Riveen's couch.

"Their own homes." Ninfa walked Riveen toward his bedroom. "All alive, though not, as much as I hate it, unharmed. None were killed."

"Oh, thank the gods," Draven muttered, collapsing onto the couch as relief swept over him. "Thank the gods. I saw deaths, saw injuries."

Ninfa stopped with Riveen in the hall. "No deaths. Andres had his lover show you things that did *not* happen."

"The...the things in the ocean, that pulled at us?" Draven asked.

Ninfa scowled. "Real. Dead now, but real. None of our family died. Some will be scarred, but that is the worst of it. No lost limbs, no deaths."

Draven's eyes burned. "Thank you."

She shook her head. "Not me, but the daughter of our maker, who worked through me." She smiled then, and a mischievous look lit her dark eyes. "As my lover, she would not let death tear my family apart."

Draven blinked as Titus gasped.

"You're — you — ?" Draven shook his head.

Ninfa shushed Riveen when he made a choked sound. "No talking. I've explained all I intend to at this moment. Be glad I have such amazing taste in mates, for she is mine, and I am hers."

Draven didn't ask anything else. Andres' lover had nearly broken his brain — as a deity, he'd been incomprehensible to the shifter mind, unable to be understood or properly seen. *Too much for mere mortals.* He wondered if Ninfa would be immortal now.

"Is Ninfa dating a demigod, or is there something…a step below a demigod?"

Draven faced Titus. "I have no idea if there is. I'm not sure I want to know."

"You've got a point," Titus agreed. "We couldn't look directly at whatever-his-name was Andres was with, and hearing him speak was painful."

"My thoughts exactly."

A sound coming from of Riveen's room had Draven starting to get up, then he felt a subtle wave of power emanating from the same direction. An unfamiliar feminine voice rumbled, and Titus chuckled.

"Well, I guess that must be Ninfa's SO?"

"Must be. At least, I hope some random person or goddess or…whatever, didn't just appear in Riveen's room." Draven wouldn't have been surprised by anything at that point.

"What a wonderful world we live in," Titus whispered.

"I love you, Titus." Draven sighed and rested his head on Titus' shoulder.

"I love you, too." Titus kissed his brow. "Always."

Before Draven could drift off there on the couch in a state of warm fuzziness, he heard Ninfa's footsteps and knew she was returning to the living room. He peeked out of one eye at her. "How bad is he?"

Ninfa sat in the rocking chair across from him. "He will be fine. Hileana is attending to him, but her power is limited since she expended so much energy earlier. She has offered to go to her father and request his help, and if that's what you want, I will tell her—but be warned that asking a favor of a deity always comes with a price."

"What price did you pay?" Draven opened his other eye.

Ninfa shook her head and smiled like a sappy, lovesick person. Draven knew he wore that same look often, too.

"None. Hileana gave her help out of love, just as I would give anything if she needed it from me. That is the nature of true love, is it not?" Ninfa started rocking slowly. "And she is capable of being around mortals, obviously. She is strong enough to control her power, unlike some other demigods who shall remain nameless...and dead. Axquital, the god of death, did not take kindly to Tokokuen's interference. Although Tokokuen had told Andres he could not kill any mortals, he should never have brought Andres back without first presenting his desire to do so to Axquital."

"I need to study up on all these deities," Draven muttered.

"It would be appreciated but it is not necessary. They always have been and always will be, at least for us. Humans have their own gods and goddesses, or the singular, depending on their beliefs. Even when one doesn't believe, that does not eradicate what will always exist." She shrugged.

The conversation was getting too complicated for Draven to follow when his body and mind screamed for sleep.

"Would you like to meet Hileana?" Ninfa asked.

Draven wasn't quite so tired. He sat up and nodded. "As long as she doesn't make our brains ache and our eyes bleed."

"I have more control than that."

Though her voice came from down the hall, Draven heard the power in every word. He shivered and slid his hand over Titus'.

"So far so good," Titus murmured.

That was true enough.

Her footsteps were light, and when she appeared, Draven was taken aback. Then he chided himself for stereotyping. He'd expected Hileana to be big, tall, powerful-looking, but she was a petite woman with light brown hair that hung in ringlets past her shoulders, and eyes the color of burnt gold.

"Not what you expected?" She quirked an eyebrow at him.

Draven didn't see the point in lying. Surely she'd know if he did. "Guilty. I shouldn't have presumed."

"True enough." Hileana crossed over to stand by Ninfa. "It's a common occurrence, however, so don't feel too bad about it."

Draven stood, with Titus' help. He felt like he should bow or something, though instead, he offered words he meant sincerely. "Thank you for saving us, for saving our family."

Hileana nodded. "You're welcome. I gladly volunteered to take on Tokokuan because of Ninfa, but had I not done so, another member of my family would have stepped in. We can't allow any level of gods or goddesses to run amok and break our laws. Humans would find out about us and find some way to destroy us. Sneaky things, you humans." She tilted her head at Titus. "You'll keep our secret, though, won't you?"

"O-of course." Titus gulped.

"I wouldn't threaten you," Hileana said. "Please don't think me so crass."

"Okay. Thanks. I guess?" Titus huffed. "I mean, thank you for helping us, and thank you for not turning me into a pile of seagull feathers. Or something."

"Feathers, hmm? I'll keep that in mind for the next shifter that annoys me." Hileana looked at Ninfa. "What do you think?"

Ninfa wrinkled her nose. "Not feathers. I like feathers. And no turning anyone into anything."

"I would never." Hileana batted her eyelashes at Ninfa.

"I know you wouldn't, love." Ninfa patted her lap, and Hileana sat.

And despite the fact that Hileana was some type of a goddess of whatever level, Draven soon found himself and Titus having a lively conversation with her and Ninfa.

As far as strange days went, this one would be at the top of the chart.

He watched Titus telling a funny story about one of his students. Titus told the story with his whole body just about, leaning forward, waving his arms, pitching his voice to mimic a child's.

As far as awesome days went, this one was also at the top of the chart. Titus was alive and unharmed, and Titus loved him, deeply, truly.

That love was the greatest gift of all.

Epilogue

Three weeks later…

"I am so fucking glad we found a place to rent until the house is rebuilt." Draven leaned against the front door after he locked it. "I love Rive, but if we'd had to stay with him for one day longer, I'd have lost my mind."

Titus couldn't help but grin. "Yeah, once you stopped fawning over him — after he threw a fit because you kept fawning over him — and after you stopped insisting that he stay in bed —"

Draven snorted and waved a hand at him. "Yeah, yeah. He just needed to get his strength back, and he wasn't going to do that running around all over."

Titus knew the depth of Draven's worry over Riveen. Despite a dose of healing from Ninfa's lover, Riveen had been weak and barely able to talk for almost a week. It'd taken another week after that before Riveen had been almost back to normal.

And the last week of staying with Riveen had just about driven Titus and Draven *both* nuts.

"Well, now we're finally in our own place, with some privacy," Titus said, trying for his sexiest voice. "And we can—"

Draven's phone blared with Riveen's ringtone.

Draven groaned and took the phone from his shirt pocket. "Gods help us all, this better be an emergency!" He tapped the screen. "You're on speaker, Rive."

"Oh, good! So I caught you two doing the nasty?"

"No," Draven groused. "We just got here."

"Damn. My timing's off. Let me hang up and call in five minutes."

"Don't you dare!" Draven looked at Titus and scowled. "Is there a reason you called, other than hoping to interrupt us having sex?"

"Hmm. Nope. I'll call back." Riveen hung up.

Draven turned his phone off. "No he won't." He pushed away from the door, his gaze locked on Titus. "And now we get to break in the rental."

Titus flushed with arousal, heat pooling in his groin. "Hmm. You think so? Maybe we should have dinner first. Or put up the groceries at least."

Draven slapped the thermostat dial as low as it'd go. "Food'll keep."

Titus' dick began to harden. Draven all prowly and toppy was the hottest thing *ever*.

"I don't know," Titus mused, trying not to sound as breathless as he felt. "The lube's in one of those bags."

Draven cursed. "Shit. Which bag?"

Titus shrugged. "Your guess is as good as mine. Of course, there's the duffel—" He yelped as Draven rushed him. "Hey!"

Draven had him in a fireman's carry before Titus could get another sound out. "Gotcha. You're all mine."

Titus slid a hand into one of Draven's back pockets and squeezed his ass. "Have been since I met you."

"Sweet man." Draven patted Titus' butt. "Sexy man."

"Wrong way round man." Not that Titus minded much. He pinched Draven's rump.

"Ow!" Draven swatted him in return.

Titus laughed. "You can't put me in this position and expect me not to play."

"We're both gonna play." Draven caressed Titus from ass to mid-thigh, then the world tilted, and Titus was sliding down the front of Draven's body.

"Mmm." Every part of Draven felt so good. Titus ran his hands over Draven's biceps, then, lower, to his waist. "Perfect." He leaned closer, gaze locking on Draven's lips.

Draven didn't disappoint. He moved one hand to Titus' nape, the other to his hip, and he kissed Titus, gently at first, a brush of lips then tongue.

Titus pressed closer, needing more contact. "Please."

Draven spun them around, then they were falling. Titus wasn't worried. He landed on the bed and Draven came down partially on him, kissing Titus in that rough, needy way he craved.

Titus clung to Draven, kissing him back, thrusting his tongue against Draven's, losing himself in the taste of his lover. He nipped Draven's tongue then sucked on it as Draven buried his hands in his hair. The hot, hard length of Draven's cock alongside Titus' seemed to burn through the layers of clothes between them.

Titus wanted their clothes gone. He squirmed, intent on getting Draven naked as soon as possible, then jolted when his cell phone chimed.

Draven raised his head and groaned. "Tell me that's not my brother calling you!"

Titus stared at Draven's lips, wet, red, swollen from kissing. He wanted to do so many things to those lips—

Draven sat astride him and took Titus' phone out of his pocket. "Should never have gotten this damn thing."

Titus blinked, then blinked again. "Huh?"

"This phone. Or we should never have let Riveen have the number." Draven poked at the screen. "Stop calling, Rive!"

"Oh! I interrupted—"

Draven turned the phone off and tossed it somewhere on the bed. He leered at Titus. "Now, where was I?"

Titus found a functioning brain cell. "Getting naked."

Draven grinned. "Sounds good to me." He slid off Titus and stood by the bed. "Whoever gets naked first gets—"

Titus whipped off his shirt, kicked off his shoes, then shoved his shorts and underwear down. He fumbled with his socks, because when he sat up to remove them, Draven tugged down his own shorts and briefs, and his cock was right *there* in front of Titus' face.

Or close enough to it.

Titus slipped off the bed and down to his knees. "Gimme." He cupped Draven's balls and used his hold to draw Draven's dick to his mouth.

Titus licked the leaking tip, tongued the slit while he rolled Draven's balls in his palm.

"Titus," Draven rasped, resting one hand on top of Titus' head and pinching his own nipple with the other. "Oh yeah, like that."

Titus licked and sucked the crown until Draven was gasping and trying to press into his mouth. He opened wide and took half of Draven's length in, came up, swirled his tongue around the glans, then went back down.

Draven hissed and his eyes nearly closed. Titus kept his gaze on Draven's face, watching his expression. When Titus pressed the tip of his tongue against Draven's slit, Draven shuddered, and his eyes fell closed as soft curses escaped him.

Titus rubbed one finger over the soft skin behind Draven's balls and took Draven's shaft into his mouth again. He flicked his tongue as he worked, and was rewarded with the flavor of pre-cum and another shudder from Draven.

Both spurred him to take Draven in deeper, to suck harder and get more of those needy sounds Draven was making. He swallowed when Draven breached his throat, came back up to tease the tip, then glided down again.

Titus could have sucked Draven until he came, but Draven cupped his chin and thrust a few times, quaking when he pressed into Titus' throat, then rubbed his thumb along the side of Titus' mouth and looked at him.

Instead of speaking, Draven knelt and pulled Titus to him. He kissed Titus, and there was an unmistakable reverence in it, tangled up with need.

Titus held on to Draven, heart filled with love that he knew would only grow stronger.

Then Draven palmed Titus' ass, kneading his cheeks and spreading them. Titus clutched at Draven, rubbing against him, bringing sweet friction to his cock. It wasn't enough, but part of the pleasure was in the need that increased with each brush of cock on cock.

Draven dipped his head down and nipped Titus' neck.

"Oh, yes," Titus whispered, goosebumps pebbling his skin. "Yes, please."

Draven began to suck on the spot he'd nipped. Titus couldn't keep still, couldn't stop thrusting, grinding, seeking more from his lover.

"Patience," Draven said against Titus' wet skin.

Titus tried to growl, but Draven's finger rubbing over his hole shorted out his speech circuit.

Draven massaged his hole and kept kissing Titus' neck and lips until Titus was dizzy with pleasure.

He thought he begged Draven to fuck him but wasn't sure the words ever made it past his lips.

Until Draven said, "Oh, I am," and maneuvered Titus around to face the bed.

Titus didn't even get to ask what was happening. He knew when Draven parted his cheeks what was coming next—and it was confirmed when Draven licked over his hole.

Titus was incoherent after the third lick, and by the time Draven was tongue-fucking him, the only sounds Titus could make were guttural grunts and moans.

"Love you," Draven said a moment later.

Titus was dimly aware of the sound of the lube being opened, the gurgle and splutter of it being poured. He moaned again when Draven worked the viscous stuff into him, slicking up Titus' hole.

Then Draven was pressing up behind Titus, the fat tip of his cock nudging his hole.

Titus arched his lower back and shoved, needing Draven's shaft in him. The head stretched him wide, caused an ache and burn, that intoxicating mix of pain and pleasure that Titus loved.

"Fuck," Draven mumbled. "I was—fuck!" He pressed in deeper, then deeper still, until he bottomed out. "God…damn. You feel so…oh…" He moved his hips in a way that sent zings of ecstasy throughout Titus.

Then he grabbed Titus by the shoulder and hip, withdrew fully, and slowly filled him again. "Fuck, honey, you should…you should see this."

Titus couldn't keep his eyes open when he was lost in the blissful feeling of having Draven fuck him. Every withdrawal, every thrust, every tightening of Draven's hands on him, every drop of sweat that fell, every rasped breath and broken curse—all served to push Titus closer to an orgasm that felt bigger than anything he'd ever experienced.

Draven began to fuck him faster, began pulling Titus back into each thrust. Titus cried out when Draven's dick rubbed over his gland. He didn't know if he managed to form a word, didn't care as he lost control and concern, as he let himself do nothing but feel and chase the pleasure being pounded into him.

Titus was wild with it, he let go on levels he never had before. He was need and want and lust, love and hunger and release.

Draven's hand on his cock intensified everything. Titus braced his arms against the bed and shoved back harder.

"Fuck!" Draven began jacking him hard and fast. "Come, come, come, Titus —"

Titus jerked, his whole body involved as he gave way to the orgasm breaking in him. His ears rang from his shout or Draven's — he didn't know which — or it could have been both. Cum jetted from his cock a moment before Draven bit down on his shoulder, the sting of pain just enough to add to the pleasure.

Draven's release warmed Titus from the inside, then he lost himself in his climax, which seemed to go on and on, turning him weak from the power of it. Titus' legs were too shaky to keep him up, and had Draven not locked his arms around him, he'd probably have just toppled over and slept for a few hours.

But Draven *did* steady him. "Titus, Titus, you have…" Draven thrust a few times before kissing Titus' nape, "You have my heart and soul."

Titus grinned. He knew he did, just like Draven knew — "And you've got mine."

And not just for a summer, but forever.

Want to see more from this author? Here's a taster for you to enjoy!

Triple Threat: Howling for More
Bailey Bradford

Coming December 2021

Excerpt

Sex. The scent of it hung heavy in the air of the club's restroom—which was probably a good thing. Bowen sighed as he leaned against one wall, nearly bumping elbows with the guy on the left of him.

Kneeling at Bowen's feet was Chiz, one of his occasional hook-ups when neither man had someone else to fuck around with.

Bowen had been in a dry spell for a few months. Work on the ranch had taken up all his time, the birthing of the foals and caring for the horses more important than his own libido.

But tonight, he needed to get off with someone else rather than all alone, and Chiz obviously felt the same way.

Chiz opened his mouth and sucked the tip of Bowen's cockhead in while looking up at Bowen through thick blond-tipped lashes. Chiz flicked his tongue, and Bowen bit back a moan. He wasn't going to last long tonight, not after how long it had been for him, and now with Chiz's very talented mouth working his dick.

Bowen braced one hand on Chiz's shoulder, the other on the wall and began to thrust, knowing it was okay to do so. Chiz's lashes fluttered, then he closed his eyes and sucked Bowen off with an enthusiasm that likely made every other man getting sucked off in the bathroom jealous.

Bowen clenched both hands, wishing he could just grab Chiz's blond hair and use it to hold his head still. Bowen liked wielding control while having sex, but it wasn't something he did often. Certainly not with one-night stands.

Though, he *had* messed around with Chiz a handful of times, at least.

Still, they weren't friends, just two guys getting off together.

But would it hurt to —

Bowen shut off that stream of thought. Now was neither the time nor place for him to decide to get all...*whatever*. He hissed as pleasure raced throughout his body. His balls drew tight, and his groin burned with the beginnings of his climax.

Chiz deep-throated him again, and that was it. Bowen let go, let his orgasm burst free and shoot in hot jets down Chiz's throat.

"I think we're gonna have us a turn at that mouth and ass."

Bowen's eyes had almost closed when he heard that comment. He slipped his hand from Chiz's shoulder to his nape, the automatic need to protect rising quickly and stomping out any lingering sexual bliss.

The bathroom had grown less crowded — except for the three men standing in a half-circle, blocking off the exit.

Bowen growled and didn't give two shits about his own cock flopping free as he tightened his clasp on Chiz. "Whatever you dumb fucks are thinking, unthink it. You ain't touching him."

The biggest man, a grizzled, ugly guy who looked like he needed a shower or three, smirked at Bowen. "And who says we was talking about *him*?"

Well, Bowen would rather avoid a fight altogether, but if those three shitheels were going to be coming after either him or Chiz, Bowen would rather be the target.

"Aw, Earl! That guy can suck dick!"

"Shut up, Killer." Earl didn't look away from Bowen.

"Killer?" Chiz muttered against Bowen's shaft. "Seriously?" He tried to turn his head.

Bowen's fight instincts were engaging. He had a feeling there'd be no easy-outs tonight.

And his daddy had always told him to get in the first punch.

The scent of danger was in the air, and Bowen couldn't ignore it, not that he would have tried. Instincts existed for a reason, or at least his did.

In a second, he had Chiz behind him and was lunging at Earl, the leader of the pack of idiots. Bowen managed to get his dick tucked into his underwear while swinging hard with his left hand.

He was fast, too fast for a burly, out-of-shape man like Earl to escape. His fist connecting with Earl's jaw felt pretty damned good.

Sex and violence…the two were linked sometimes. Bowen wouldn't examine that very closely, not if he could help it.

Earl's head jerked to the side. Blood and spit flew from his mouth as all hell broke loose in the restroom.

And maybe Bowen should have thought out his attack a little better, because Earl didn't go down, and his two buddies shot past Bowen.

He had to protect Chiz—Chiz was small-boned, almost delicately built, and all three men were...none of those things.

Bowen kicked Earl in the balls, and the big fool went down with a high-pitched screech. Bowen spun around and grabbed both men by the backs of their shirts. He pulled and ripped the material, then had to grab at them again.

One of them—Killer, he thought—went flying backward. The other, Bowen clutched at, spun around then punched in the gut.

Bowen caught a flash of Chiz shooting up and lunging away. At first, Bowen thought Chiz was running for the door.

But no. Killer was flung against the wall beside the man Bowen was trying to take down.

Chiz was there, moving so fast with punches and martial arts moves that Bowen couldn't keep up with what he was doing.

Especially not when Bowen nearly got kneed in the balls.

He focused on the fight he was in, avoiding damage to his family jewels, taking a hard slug to the ribs, then elbowing his opponent in the gut before using an uppercut to finally take the fucker out.

By then, Chiz was standing, hands on his slender hips, tapping one foot.

Bowen looked at him head-on.

Chiz nodded. "Wasn't sure if you'd need help."

Bowen almost laughed at that. He'd held back a lot of his strength since he didn't want to end up in prison for murder.

Chiz scowled at him. "I can take care of myself. I'm not some delicate flower, here."

"Yeah, I get that, but maybe we should leave before these fuckwits regain consciousness?" Bowen suggested. His knuckles burned, the skin raw and abraded, but it'd be healed up in no time at all.

"Probably." Chiz wrinkled his nose as he glanced at the men. "Ugh. I hope they aren't thinking they'll be regulars here." Then he canted his head and grinned at Bowen. "And I didn't get to come. I'm pretty sure you're not a psycho-serial killer, so, um, if you want to go back to my place, we could do that."

Bowen's first impulse was to say no, but he checked it. First things first—he and Chiz needed to get out of there.

"Come on." Bowen took Chiz by the elbow.

"Not a delicate flower," Chiz muttered, but he didn't pull away.

"Nah, you kicked ass. What were you doing?" Bowen asked as he led Chiz out of the restroom.

"Fighting," Chiz replied. "Duh."

Bowen cut him a narrow look. "Anyone ever spanked you?"

"I refuse to answer that," Chiz drawled, "on account of I'd have to explain where the bodies were. Hypothetically, of course."

That startled a laugh out of Bowen. "Is that so? 'Cause I think you'd like it."

"Right. The younger, delicate little twink—"

"You got a hang-up over that delicate part," Bowen observed, interrupting Chiz while opening the restroom door. "Don't ya?"

Chiz sniffed and pulled his arm free. "Do not."

Bowen laughed again. How was it he hadn't known Chiz was so feisty?

'Cause all I've ever seen him as is a way to get off. Wow. I'm an asshole. Though, to be fair, I don't think Chiz's seen me any differently.

The club was still packed, but several people looked their way when Bowen and Chiz left the restroom. Bowen's anger sparked. "Those fuckin' assholes watching us knew we were gonna be jumped."

"Probably," Chiz agreed. "A pox on all of them. May their urethras be inflamed and burn with the stings of a thousand wasps."

"Fuck." That made Bowen's dick ache.

Chiz grinned. "I could flip them off, if you want to fight some more?"

"Rather not." Bowen's pulse escalated, not at the idea of fighting, but at the mischievous way Chiz was acting. He was *interesting*, not just attractive.

Chiz shrugged. "Okay, your call. You wanna come back to mine? I'd like to get off a few times tonight."

Oh damn! A few times? How stupid had Bowen been, not chatting with Chiz more until now?

"Yeah, let's do that." Bowen licked his suddenly dry lips. He'd just come not five minutes ago, and he was already close to getting hard again.

Chiz winked at him. "Cool. Maybe I'll let you slap my ass a time or two."

That was a gauntlet thrown down. Bowen ghosted a hand over Chiz's ass. "Maybe I'll let you beg me to."

Chiz narrowed his eyes at Bowen. "*Beg you to?*"

But Chiz's pulse sped up. Bowen could see it fluttering at the base of his neck and he noted the flare of Chiz's nostrils and the beginning of an erection pressing against the fly of his pants.

"What the hell's going on?" roared someone from the back of the club. Literally, Bowen thought, from the back, where there might be offices or something. He didn't know. He just came there to get laid and wasn't buddies with anyone.

"Seems like a good time to split," Chiz said. He grasped Bowen's hand. "Because that sounds like one pissed-off man, and I've heard stories about the guy who owns this place."

"Oh?" Bowen was curious, but Chiz tugged, and Bowen followed.

"Yup, and you don't want to fight any more tonight, right?"

"Right." Bowen would much rather fuck, and Chiz was...*interesting*.

PUBLISHING

Sign up for our newsletter and find out about all our romance book releases, eBook sales and promotions, sneak peeks and FREE romance books!

About the Author

A native Texan, Bailey spends her days spinning stories around in her head, which has contributed to more than one incident of tripping over her own feet. Evenings are reserved for pounding away at the keyboard, as are early morning hours. Sleep? Doesn't happen much. Writing is too much fun, and there are too many characters bouncing about, tapping on Bailey's brain demanding to be let out.

Caffeine and chocolate are permanent fixtures in Bailey's office and are never far from hand at any given time. Removing either of those necessities from Bailey's presence can result in what is known as A Very, Very Scary Bailey and is not advised under any circumstances.

Bailey loves to hear from readers. You can find her contact information, website details and author profile page at https://www.pride-publishing.com